HENRY REED, INC.

ALSO BY KEITH ROBERTSON

THE WRECK OF THE *Saginaw*
THREE STUFFED OWLS
THE CROW AND THE CASTLE
HENRY REED'S JOURNEY
HENRY REED'S BABY-SITTING SERVICE
THE YEAR OF THE JEEP
THE MONEY MACHINE
HENRY REED'S BIG SHOW

HENRY REED, INC.

BY KEITH ROBERTSON
ILLUSTRATED BY ROBERT McCLOSKEY

THE VIKING PRESS · NEW YORK

PRINTED IN U.S.A. BY THE VAIL-BALLOU PRESS, INC.

HENRY REED, INC.

Sunday morning, June 23rd

My name is Henry Harris Reed and this is my journal. It is my private property and in case that it gets lost, please return it to me in care of my uncle, Mr. J. Alfred Harris, RD 1, Grover's Corner, Princeton, N.J.

This is a journal, not a diary. Diaries are kept by girls and tell all about their dates and what they think of their different boy friends. My mother says that men keep diaries too, that the most famous diary in the world was kept a long time ago by an Englishman named Pepys. That may be so, but when I read about pirates and explorers and sea captains they always keep journals, so this is going to be a journal. It is going to be a record of what happens to me this summer in New Jersey.

First I had better explain why I'm keeping a journal. My father is in the diplomatic service, and has been as long as I can remember. Right now he's a consul stationed at the consular office in Naples, Italy, and I go to the American school there. There are a lot of American students of my age in Naples. Most of them are the sons and daughters of Navy officers, Army officers, and Air Force officers who are on duty over there. Some have been away from the United States for a year, some for two years, and some, like me, most of their lives. Of course, I've visited the United States a number of times, so it's not really strange to me.

There are three in my class, which will be the eighth grade when school opens again, who are coming to the United States for the summer and expect to go back this fall. Miss Prescott, our history and government teacher, asked us to keep notes on our experiences and to tell the class about them when school starts again. She said if we do a good job we won't have to make the two book reports that her students ordinarily make.

Miss Prescott also wants us to report on how students our age earn spending money in the United States. She suggested that we might want to get jobs ourselves such as mowing lawns and baby sitting and things like that. If possible she'd like us to do something that can be used to illustrate "free enterprise."

Mildred Doyle is going to spend the summer with her grandmother in Vermont. If she gets all the new clothes that she claims she's going to get, she'll spend the summer sitting around with her hands folded in her lap, looking at herself in the mirror, and she won't have much that's interesting to tell our class. Chesty Robbins is going to St. Louis for the summer. He'll probably do a lot of interesting things but he'll be too lazy to keep any record, and even if he wasn't lazy he doesn't know how to spell well

8

enough to keep much of a journal. I guess if anyone is going to make a decent report to the class it will have to be me. I'll do my best. I'll put down things just as they happen so I'll have a complete record when I get back.

I arrived in New York day before yesterday to stay with an aunt and uncle I hadn't seen since I was very young and didn't remember much about. I came over with Mr. and Mrs. Hunter, who are friends of my father and mother. There's not much point in telling about my trip across the ocean because everyone in my class has been across the ocean at least once. They had to cross it to get to Italy from the United States. Some of us, like me, have been across eight or ten times, and now we think crossing the ocean is a bore. I'll leave my trip out and start with the interesting part of my summer, which is when I arrived in Princeton last night.

The Hunters put me on a train in New York at Pennsylvania Station and my Aunt Mabel and Uncle Al met me at Princeton Junction. The train was supposed to get in at six-thirty but it was almost half an hour late. Aunt Mabel asked me if I was hungry and I said I was. She suggested that we have dinner at the Princeton Inn and Uncle Al agreed.

My Aunt Mabel is a big woman, about fifty-five I suppose, with gray hair and a nice, friendly smile. She loves to eat but she is always trying not to because she says she's overweight. Uncle Al likes his food too, and he has a great

9

big stomach, big, heavy cheeks, and about three chins. He's almost completely bald and what little hair he does have is white. Both he and my Aunt Mabel are sort of slow, easy-going, good-natured people and I liked them both right away.

We ordered our dinner at the Princeton Inn and while we were waiting for it to come they asked me how my mother and father were, and what sort of trip I'd had, and things like that. Uncle Al kept looking at me and shaking his head now and then.

"You're the spitting image of your mother," he said. "I just can't get over it. It sort of gives me a shock every time I look at you."

"I don't see much resemblance," Aunt Mabel said.

"Perhaps not with the way Jane looks now," Uncle Al said. "I'm thinking about the way she looked when she was a girl. If you gave him long hair and put a dress on him he could be Jane sitting there when she was thirteen or fourteen. She had that same serious, intent look, she wore horn-rimmed spectacles just like his, and her eyes and his are identical."

No one had ever accused me of looking like a girl before, but I'm used to relatives making silly remarks about how much I've grown, who I look like, and where I get my hair and eyes. My father's folks always claim I look like his side of the family, and now here was Uncle Al swearing that I look like my mother. I didn't mind particularly because I like the way my mother looks.

"I think it's wonderful that you were able to come spend the summer with us," Aunt Mabel said, "and I hope you'll enjoy it. I'm a little worried, though, that you may find it sort of dull. In fact, since reading your mother's last letter, I've felt a trifle guilty because I haven't given her more information."

11

"I don't know why you should," Uncle Al said. "After all, she grew up at Grover's Corner."

"I know," Aunt Mabel said. "But she left here fifteen years ago, and things have changed. You see, Henry, where we live, which is about three miles from Princeton, there's only a little cluster of nine houses. Everything around is farm land."

"Which would you rather be called, Henry or Hank?" Uncle Al asked.

"Hank," I replied.

"According to what Al tells me," Aunt Mabel said, "when your mother was a girl at Grover's Corner almost every one of these nine houses was filled with children. Now there are only two families that have any at all. The Glasses have a daughter about your age, perhaps a little younger, and the Cassidys have two boys aged thirteen and fifteen."

"Are they fun?" I asked.

"I guess so. They're noisy, at least," Aunt Mabel replied. "Unfortunately it doesn't make much difference. They've both gone to camp and will be away the entire summer. I'm afraid that we can't promise you much in the way of playmates. I'll have to speak to some of the women I know in the garden club and see if they know of any boys your age."

I could see that she was really worried about the situation and the last thing I wanted was for her to go scouting around trying to find boys for me to play with. When grownups do that they always pick someone who is about as interesting as a plate of cold spaghetti and then they wonder why you don't appreciate all the trouble they've gone to.

"I'll find lots of things to do," I told her. "It's going to be fun just being in the country. We've always lived in some city or other."

"That's right. I guess you have," Uncle Al agreed. He cocked his head to one side and looked at me sharply. "Do you like animals, fish, bugs, and things like that?"

"I'm going to be a naturalist when I grow up," I told him.

"Do you like snakes?" he asked.

"I had a pet one for quite a while when we lived in London."

"How about birds?"

"All I've got are four or five Java finches now," I said. "I had quite a few that I got at the bird market in Paris but they caught pneumonia on the train and died when we moved to Naples."

Uncle Al shook his head, pursed his lips, and blew out his breath in sort of a half-whistle. "Talk about heredity," he said, "look at him. He's not only the spitting image of his mother and talks like her, but he's interested in the same thing. Boys are supposed to be the ones who come

13

home with their pockets full of worms and birds' eggs and bugs, but in our family it was your mother. She was going to be a naturalist, too. She caught butterflies, she fed every baby bird that dropped out of its nest, she had an aquarium with ninety-nine different kinds of fish, and her bedroom was practically a menagerie. One day she caught three hundred and forty-four crickets. Whatever she planned to do with them I've no idea. Maybe she was trying to set some kind of a record or maybe she was going to feed something she had hidden in her closet. Anyhow, on the way upstairs she dropped the box and they all got out. What a night that was! You never heard such a chirping in all your life. I don't think one of us got a wink of sleep."

He leaned back in his chair and roared with laughter until his eyes began to water. Then he took out a big handkerchief and blew his nose and wiped his eyes. "Amazing!" he said. "And frightening, too."

"What is?" I asked.

"I was just talking to myself," he replied. "I don't think we need worry too much about other boys your age. You'll find lots to do out where we live if you're going to be a naturalist."

By the time we had finished dinner it was dark, and I didn't see much of Princeton as we drove home. We were outside town about a mile, driving along a black-top road, when Uncle Al began to slow down. "Look at that!"

14

he said. "There's a dog right there in the middle of the road."

I was in the back seat but I could see between him and Aunt Mabel. Sure enough, sitting right in the middle of our side of the road was a dog. He was small, mainly white with some black and brown spots, and with long floppy ears. For a minute I thought he might be dead. Then he turned his head and seemed to be looking straight at us. Uncle Al went slower and slower and finally came to a stop about twenty-five feet from the dog.

"I wonder what's wrong with him," he said.

"I'll get out and see," I volunteered.

"I don't know if that's wise," Aunt Mabel said doubtfully. "You can't tell about a strange dog. It might be vicious."

I had the door open and was out of the car before she finished. "I'll be careful," I promised. "Besides, dogs usually like me." I walked around in front of the car and said, "Hello, boy. How are you?" The dog wagged his tail and stood up. He was a short, stumpy dog and his tail stood straight up in the air. His face was sad and mournful but his eyes were very intelligent. He wagged his tail and gave a little yip to show that he knew I was speaking to him.

"Come here, boy," I called. "Come on."

He came trotting toward me but instead of stopping as I expected, he went right on past me toward the back of the car. I started after him, but after I passed the front fender there wasn't much light; I couldn't see what had become of him.

"He's disappeared!" I said.

"Well, he's out of the middle of the road and he seems to be all right. Come on, hop in," Uncle Al said.

I climbed in the car, slammed the door, and sat down in the middle of the back seat as before. Then something cold touched my wrist. I jumped and turned my head to look. The dog was sitting on the seat beside me.

"He got in the car!" I said.

Uncle Al had started forward but he stopped the car again. He reached back and flipped on the overhead light. "Well, can you beat that!" he said. "Nervy little cuss, isn't he?"

"It's a beagle," said Aunt Mabel. "And a very nice little beagle."

"Beagles are hunting dogs, aren't they?" I asked.

"Rabbit dogs," Uncle Al said, agreeing. "Open the door, will you, Hank, and see if you can coax him out?"

"Why don't you look at his collar first?" Aunt Mabel suggested. "Maybe that'll tell you who he belongs to."

The dog was wearing an old brown leather collar which I examined all the way around. There was no license tag on it and no name plate.

"The poor thing's probably lost," Aunt Mabel said.

"Well, if we take him with us in the car he's liable to

16

be lost even further," said Uncle Al. "I think the best thing to do is to leave him where we found him. Maybe he'll find his way back or his owner will locate him."

I opened the right-hand door again and got out. "Here, boy," I called. "Come on, outside." The dog wagged his tail, sort of grinned at me, and sat where he was.

I called again three or four times, but the dog apparently had no intention of getting out of the car. Finally, Uncle Al got tired of waiting and got out on his side. He opened the back door opposite me, reached in, grabbed the dog by the nape of his neck, and set him down in the road. Almost instantly the dog began to howl. I've heard lots of howls, but his is the most mournful one I've ever heard. You would have thought he was starving, freezing, and being beaten to death all at once. He pointed his nose up at the sky and let go with everything he had. With a beagle that's plenty.

"Oh, be quiet," Uncle Al said. "Come on, Hank, let's go."

"You aren't going to drive off and leave him in the middle of the road again, are you?" Aunt Mabel asked. "Why, he'll be killed!"

"He won't be if he's got sense enough to move out of the middle," said Uncle Al.

"The poor thing is lost and lonesome and confused," Aunt Mabel insisted.

"And noisy," Uncle Al added.

"At least, you ought to see that he gets off to one side of the road," she said. "That's only ordinary decency."

Uncle Al had started forward, so once more he stopped and began backing up. I looked out of the back window and told him when to stop.

"See if you can coax him over to one side of the road," Aunt Mabel suggested.

I opened the door and got out on the side of the road nearest the ditch. I circled around the back of the car, and as I approached the beagle he darted past me and disappeared around the right rear wheel. I'd left the car door open again and I had a pretty good idea where he'd gone. I had had only a couple of glimpses of the dog but I liked him. He was a smart little hound and knew what he wanted. I like all dogs, but I have to admit that a lot of them are dumb. It's only once in a long time that you find a really smart dog. It looked as though we had found one, or rather he had found us.

"Where'd he go?" I called.

"He's back in the car again," Uncle Al replied, sounding a little tired of it all.

I reached the door and turned on the light again. There was the beagle sitting up in the back seat, holding out his paws in front of him as though he were begging.

"Isn't he cute?" Aunt Mabel asked.

"Just darling," said Uncle Al with a shake of his head.

"If we leave him here he's going to get killed," Aunt

18

Mabel said. "I think we should take him home with us."

"I don't," Uncle Al said, "for three reasons. First, the owner might come by here and find him if we leave him where he is. He's never going to find him at our place. Second, the dog got here somehow, probably on foot, and he may be able to find his way back. It won't help him any to take him two or three miles in the car. He'll never be able to back-trail then."

There was a pause, and then Aunt Mabel asked, "What's the third reason?"

Uncle Al just chuckled to himself.

"What is it, Al?" Aunt Mabel insisted.

"I'm just afraid of establishing a pattern," Uncle Al said. "Don't ask me what I mean. It's a long and harrowing story."

"Oh," Aunt Mabel said. But I could tell from the tone of her voice that she didn't know what he meant any more than I did. He had made several mysterious statements during the evening that I'll have to figure out when I have time. Also, he laughed at a couple of things that weren't funny at all.

"We can take him home and keep him overnight and bring him back tomorrow," I suggested.

"That's an excellent idea," my Aunt Mabel said.

"All right," Uncle Al said, getting in. "Hank, I guess you've got yourself a dog."

We drove on for about half a mile and then Uncle Al

began chuckling to himself again. The radio wasn't turned on and no one had said anything that was funny.

"What is it?" Aunt Mabel asked.

"You know, Hank, your Aunt Mabel and I had just one child," Uncle Al said, for no reason at all.

"Yes—Cousin Margaret, the one that's married now," I said, wondering if he thought I was stupid or something.

"Yes. Well, she was a quiet little girl, used to play with dolls and baby carriages, and things like that," Uncle Al said. "It's going to be quite a treat for your Aunt Mabel to have a boy around for a change."

When we got home Aunt Mabel found a short length of rope, which I tied to the beagle's collar. He seemed to know we were home and he jumped right out of the car without any argument. Then Uncle Al had me lead him over to the tool shed and we locked him in there for the night.

I had two big, heavy suitcases. With Uncle Al carrying one and me the other, he led the way upstairs. Behind us came Aunt Mabel. We went down a short hall and then turned on the light in a big, cheery bedroom. After Uncle Al had set his suitcase on the floor he reached over and lifted mine.

"Look at that!" he said. "His is heavier than the one I carried. He's half my size, yet he hasn't turned a hair and I'm puffing like a steam engine. Ah, youth!"

"It isn't youth so much as not being overweight," Aunt Mabel said, coming in. "I'm puffing too and I'm not carrying anything at all except a layer of fat."

She turned down the bed and bustled around the room while Uncle Al pulled a pipe out of his pocket and lighted it.

"You see those two rows of books over there on those shelves?" he asked, pointing across the room. "Those belonged to your mother. They're what she called her nature library. Those brown ones that look alike are a nature encyclopedia. Twenty volumes of spiders, birds, animals, reptiles, grasses, and butterflies. Well, you look at them yourself."

"I imagine you're tired," Aunt Mabel said, "after all the traveling you've been doing."

I wasn't particularly tired. When you travel the thing you do most is sit. All I'd been doing for three or four days was sit down either in an airplane, on a train, in a car, or someplace. For some reason or other people always expect you to say you're tired after you've traveled.

Aunt Mabel opened the closet door and showed me all the hangers and I said I thought I'd unpack some of my clothes.

Aunt Mabel put my stuff away in the bureau while I hung up the suits and trousers in the closet. Uncle Al sat on the blanket chest and watched. We were just about finished when there was a high-pitched, mournful howl from the tool shed. The shed was at least fifty feet from the house but that howl sounded as though the dog were standing right beneath the window. Aunt Mabel looked uncomfortable and Uncle Al didn't say a word. He just sat on the blanket chest and continued smoking. There was a short pause and then there was a second howl. Still no one said anything about it. With the third howl that beagle really hit his stride. The glass in the window beside the bed began to vibrate.

"He's not very happy," I said.

"So it would seem," Uncle Al replied.

"Do you think if we opened the door of the shed so he could wander around the yard it would help?" Aunt Mabel asked.

"No," Uncle Al replied, "but I'm willing to try."

"I'll go down and open the door," I volunteered.

"There's a flashlight on the kitchen table," said Uncle Al.

I went down and out the back door and opened the door to the shed. The beagle came trotting out. He didn't jump up on me or make any fuss. He just wagged his tail and trotted along at my heels as I went back toward the kitchen door. He looked up at me when I reached the door, as if asking for permission to go in. He is certainly a smart little dog.

"No," I said. "You stay out here."

I went back upstairs and was just inside the door of

22

my room when he started howling again. This time, since he was practically underneath my window, the noise was even louder than before. The whole room seemed to shake with it.

"What on earth is the matter with that dog?" my Aunt Mabel asked in an annoyed voice.

"I think maybe he's decided he likes Hank's room," Uncle Al said. That was sort of a silly statement, because of course the dog had never been up in my room.

"I don't like the idea of a stray dog in the house," said Aunt Mabel. "He might have fleas. At least he should have a bath."

"It's kind of late to give him one tonight," Uncle Al said. "It looks like the choice is between fleas or noise. We don't know that he has fleas and we do know that he howls."

"Maybe he's hungry," Aunt Mabel said. "I'll go down and see if I can find him something to eat."

I don't know much about beagles but I do know something about howls, and that wasn't a hungry howl. But I didn't say anything. Aunt Mabel and Uncle Al went downstairs to the kitchen while I changed into my pajamas. As I was getting undressed I noticed a book on the shelf about dogs so I got it down and looked up beagles.

The book didn't tell me much except that beagles were a very old breed and nobody knew exactly where they

23

originated. The author thought that there was some fox-hound in them and possibly some bloodhound. Anyhow, they are supposed to be very companionable dogs, and to be very intelligent, and to have a sharp sense of smell. The book didn't say a thing about their howling at night, but it did say they had a wonderful musical bay when they were following a rabbit. I put on my bathrobe and went downstairs to the kitchen. The beagle was finishing some food that Aunt Mabel had given him. He looked up at me and wagged his tail.

"That's a smart dog," Uncle Al said. "He's got you spotted."

"Well, now that he's had something to eat let's try him again," Aunt Mabel said. She held open the kitchen screen and said, "Come on, outside, doggie. Outside you go."

The beagle went outside as politely as could be. I looked through the screen and saw him lie down at the foot of the steps. We turned out the light and left the kitchen for the living room.

"Shall we wait down here in the living room or shall we come back down again?" Uncle Al asked.

Aunt Mabel looked at the clock. "We might as well listen to the news."

Uncle Al turned on the television and found a news program. We had listened for about four or five minutes when the beagle began to howl again.

"Well, you might as well go get him," Uncle Al said. "See if he'll keep quiet in your room."

I went to the back door and opened it and the beagle came right in. He followed me down the hall and across the living room to the stairs.

"I think I'll go to bed," I said.

"Goodnight, Hank," said Uncle Al. "It's nice having you with us."

"You sleep as late as you want to in the morning," Aunt Mabel said. "We're not planning on going to church since this is your first day here and you'll want to look around and get used to things."

The beagle followed me upstairs and into my room. He curled up on a little rag rug near the foot of my bed and promptly went to sleep.

I'd been asleep about an hour, I guess, when I woke up. I was thirsty so I got up and went down the hall to the bathroom for a drink of water. There were no lights downstairs, but Uncle Al and Aunt Mabel must have just gone to bed because I could hear them talking in their bedroom. I got my drink of water and came back out into the hall. There was a funny noise and I stood there for a minute trying to figure out what it was. Then I figured out that it was Uncle Al chuckling to himself.

"What is it?" Aunt Mabel asked in a sleepy voice.

"I was thinking about your worrying that this would be a quiet summer," Uncle Al said.

I went on down the corridor to my room. The beagle was still near the foot of my bed, snoring peacefully. I climbed into bed but I couldn't get to sleep for a while. I used the time trying to think up a good name for the dog. I decided to call him Agony.

Sunday night, June 23rd

Today has been sort of a lazy day. I got up about eight o'clock and went downstairs and had breakfast. Aunt Mabel is a really good cook. I ate two waffles, four slices of bacon, and a pear. After breakfast, I started my journal and brought it up to date. I read the funny papers and then I went outside to look around the yard. Uncle Al came out in a minute and started showing me around. He and Aunt Mabel have a big lot with a large lawn and a big vegetable garden next to it. There is a two-car garage beside the house, the tool shed where we had locked Agony last night, and a little building beyond that once was a chicken house.

There is only one car in the garage and the other half is occupied by the neatest little garden tractor I've ever seen. It is only about three feet high and about four feet long and looks like a toy. However it's a real tractor and Uncle Al started it up and put it through its paces. He looked like an elephant riding a mouse on that little tiny tractor, but it hauled him around all right. He has a lawn-mower, a sickle bar, a cart, a plow, and a cultivator that he can attach to the tractor. I told him I thought it was a wonderful outfit.

"Well, it's another version of electric trains," he said. "Only this cuts grass, so you can persuade yourself that you spent your money sensibly."

"Can I cut the lawn?" I asked him.

Uncle Al is nice but he's sort of peculiar. He likes to talk in riddles and now and then he seems to be talking to someone who isn't there. When I asked him about cutting the lawn he acted as though talking to someone else and said, "There you are. A few years ago I had to pay a dollar or a dollar and a half to have my lawn mowed. Now with

an investment of a mere nine hundred dollars this young man asks me to let him cut the lawn as a favor."

He got off the tractor and said, "Come on. We'll take a walk and I'll show you the heart of downtown Grover's Corner."

Grover's Corner is just as Aunt Mabel said it was. It isn't a town at all but nine houses built sort of close together. There are five houses on the opposite side of the road and four on the side where Uncle Al lives. There aren't any sidewalks, and we walked on the edge of the black-top road. As we walked along he told me who lived in each house but naturally I didn't remember all of the names. All the houses had big lots, and between the last two on Uncle Al's side of the road there was an extra-large lot with nothing on it except a red barn set back about twenty feet from the road.

"This is your property," Uncle Al said. "Starting from that tree there at the edge of McDaniel's lawn on over to that row of evergreens. I guess there's about four hundred feet frontage."

"What do you mean, my property?" I asked him.

"It belongs to your mother," Uncle Al replied.

"You mean she owns it?"

"That's exactly what I mean. You see, your grandfather and grandmother, and before them your great-grandfather and grandmother, and even before them your great-great-grandfather and grandmother lived here. Every-

29

thing on this side of the road was part of the old homestead. The original house sat back in the field a ways. Your grandmother and grandfather built a new house up here. It stood just to the right of that small bush there. Your mother and I grew up in that house. By the time we were kids, my folks—that's your grandparents—had sold three lots here on this side of the road. All the present houses were here except that red brick one which you can see over those evergreens. That belongs to Mr. Apple. All the houses on the opposite side of the road have been here for some time too, except one. When Mabel and I got married we bought the house that we now have. About seventeen or eighteen years ago the house that was here burned to the ground. A man came along a year or so later and wanted to dump some dirt and covered up the basement. So there you are. There's nothing but the land left, but that's where your mother and I grew up."

"How does she happen to own it?" I asked.

"Well, when your grandparents died we sold what remained of the farm. Your mother said she'd like to keep these four acres and that someday she and your father might retire here. Naturally they'd have to build a new house."

We walked on into the lot, which was overgrown with weeds. Uncle Al pointed to two big broad-breasted pigeons sitting on top of the barn.

"Those two pigeons are descendants of some of the

30

pigeons your mother used to have," he said. "She had some Silver Kings and she had some homing pigeons. They've all been mixed now and they've crossed with ordinary barn pigeons but you can still see quite a bit of the original strains that she raised. The upper part of the barn is filled with them."

We walked over to the barn and went inside. "It really isn't a barn at all," Uncle Al explained, "but an old carriage house with a ground floor and a second floor with a regular stairway."

I went upstairs while Uncle Al waited down below. There wasn't much up there but a bunch of pigeons, as Uncle Al had said. They were quite tame. Some of them flew out the broken window at one end but most of them sat where they were, looking at me. There were nests all over the place and in some of them I could see squabs peeking over the edge. I could see that it would be no trick at all to catch all the pigeons you wanted.

There wasn't much on the ground floor either, except a few barrels and boxes and some old discarded pieces of furniture. Back in one corner there was a stack of white boxes which I wouldn't have noticed if Uncle Al hadn't pointed them out.

"Beehives," he said. "Your mother used to keep bees."

"My mother kept bees!"

"She certainly did," Uncle Al replied. "At one time or another your mother kept everything that flew, crawled,

31

walked, wriggled, or swam. She had bees for quite a while. In that wooden box beside the beehives is all her old bee equipment."

I went back to take a look. Sure enough, there was a helmet with an old net hanging down from it, a pair of leather gloves that were so hard and brittle that they were like shingles, some tools, and an odd-looking contraption that looked like a fireplace bellows.

"What's this?" I asked.

"I think that was the smoke apparatus. When the bees got too active she gave them a shot of smoke. I don't believe they use those any more. There's a beekeeper over near Dutch Neck and I happened to drop by there one day while he was working with a hive. They have canned smoke now. It comes in these Aerosol cans under pressure, just like shaving cream."

There wasn't anything else in the barn to see, so we went back outside. About two acres of the front part of the lot are clear except for two or three large trees. The back part is all timber.

"You'll find racoons, possum, and now and then a deer back in those woods," Uncle Al said.

Agony had been with us from the minute we left the house. Part of the time he trotted along at my heels and part of the time he went exploring. While we were in the barn, looking around, he went sniffing off through the high weeds. As we came out the door he let out a bay that scared me half out of my wits. In fact, I didn't know what it was.

"That's the beagle on the trail of something," Uncle Al said. "For a little dog, a beagle can make a bigger noise than anything I know."

Agony didn't go chasing off anyplace but stayed pretty much in one spot. We went over to investigate. He was circling around and around a big box turtle.

"That's a fine state of affairs," Uncle Al said. "You're supposed to chase rabbits, not turtles. I don't know how you ever got far enough from your home to get lost if that's the kind of game you chase."

I picked up the turtle, which had drawn itself into its shell as tight as a bank vault. "He's a nice one," I said. "I think I'll take him home."

"I could have predicted that," Uncle Al said. "Do you know what to feed him?"

"Vegetables and berries mainly," I said. "Although turtles eat certain kinds of grubs and slugs. They'll eat raw meat too."

"By the time you get through training him, I expect the farmers around here will have to shut up their beef cattle at night," Uncle Al said. I think he was just kidding me.

I took the turtle home and put him in the chicken yard.

"You're shooting about par, I would say," Uncle Al observed. "One dog and one turtle and you haven't been

33

here twenty-four hours yet. By the way, we've got to do something about this dog."

"Why?" I asked, looking at Agony, who was busy investigating a big spider on the side of the chicken house.

"Well, he obviously belonged to someone. He looks well fed and he's wearing a collar. It seems improbable, but someone may be quite fond of him and be worrying about him. I know you'd like to keep him, but we ought to make some effort to return him to his real owner."

I could see what Uncle Al meant. Somebody else might like Agony just as much as I did, although I doubted it. "What do you think we should do?" I asked.

"I guess the best thing is to put an advertisement in the paper. If his owner is worried about him, he'll probably be watching the Lost and Found section."

"Beagles are valuable dogs," I said. "Someone who doesn't own him at all might claim him."

"That is a risk we'll have to run," Uncle Al said. "However, it needn't be too much of a risk. The only reason the dog would have much value to anyone besides the real owner is that he might be a fine, well-trained hunting dog. We can write up an advertisement that doesn't stress his hunting abilities. I doubt if we need to bend the truth much. If the true owner wants him back he'll investigate regardless of what we say."

"I'll write the advertisement," I said as we went into the house.

"All right. You do that and I'll write a note to the paper telling them to charge it to me," Uncle Al said. "Here's an old copy of the paper. You'll find some advertisements that you can use for models."

I took the paper up to my room and read a dozen or so of the classified advertisements. Some of the "Found" ones said that the owner of the property could have it back by paying for the cost of the advertisement. That seems reasonable to me. I don't see why a finder should lose money after he's gone to the trouble of finding something and saving it for a careless owner. This is what I wrote:

Found—one beagle, white with brown and black markings, on Carter Road, the night of June 22nd. Trained to chase turtles. Howls at night unless allowed to sleep in bedroom. Big eater. Owner can have by identifying and paying for this ad plus whatever dog food he has eaten. Princeton 3-6122.

That seemed a fairly accurate description. I went downstairs to show it to Uncle Al, but he wasn't around. An envelope was on his desk, addressed to the *Princeton Bugle,* and his note was inside. I folded my advertisement and stuck it in the envelope too and sealed it.

After lunch Uncle Al suggested that we go for a ride. He wanted to show me something of the Princeton area.

"You've done a lot of traveling," he said as we drove

along. "Probably a lot more than Mabel and I will ever do. You've been to a lot of places in Europe and a good many places in South America. I've forgotten just where all you have been. Anyhow you've seen a lot, but I doubt if you've ever seen an area that is a nicer place to live than right here around Princeton. Travel is supposed to be broadening, but I wouldn't be surprised if it wasn't a handicap to travel too much. It's kind of nice to spend a good many years in one spot and to get to know everybody and the countryside, to watch a community grow. The Princeton area is not only a wonderful place to live but it has a wonderful future. Right now it's one of the research centers of the world and it's growing all the time."

My Uncle Al is in the insurance business—not life insurance but fire insurance, liability insurance, automobile insurance, things like that. Naturally he gets around a lot and knows a lot about the businesses in and around Princeton. He knew what everything was and he proceeded to tell me. Uncle Al is big and heavy and slow, and he talks just the way he looks. He told me a lot more about Princeton than I wanted to know, and certainly a lot more than Aunt Mabel wanted to know, because she half went to sleep. But now and then he would say something interesting and I'm sort of used to listening to a lot of talk to get an interesting fact once in a while. We have diplomats out to our house to dinner quite often,

36

and if anybody can talk longer than a diplomat without getting to the point I don't know who it is.

According to Uncle Al the Princeton area is filled with all sorts of research centers. I didn't know that the big companies had separate buildings and places where their scientists developed new products, but apparently they do. I guess that's an example of free enterprise, and I am going to learn more about these research places in order to tell my class about them. There are several electronic-research centers near Princeton, an atomic reactor, an aircraft-development center, a textile-research center, and dozens and dozens of others.

"All these places employ chemists, scientists, engineers, and physicists," Uncle Al explained. "And besides all these there are all the professors at Princeton University, and the men at the Institute of Advanced Study. Why, there are more great brains around Princeton than there are cockroaches. There are so many brain waves given off around here it's a wonder you can't see them. Maybe somebody flying over Princeton could." He paused a minute, looked at me, and said, "I know a couple of boys out at the airport. I think I'll have to ask them someday."

Although Uncle Al is my mother's brother he resembles my father more than he does my mother. My father makes remarks like that. You're not quite certain what he means. Even my mother is confused now and then

37

by things that my father says. Often she'll stop and look at him and say, "Just what do you mean by that, Franklin?" Then Dad will chuckle just the way Uncle Al does. Mother says that Dad talks in riddles lots of times, but Dad says that there's a corner missing from her block of humor. That isn't so at all. I think Mother has a good sense of humor and mine is just like hers.

Anyhow, it appears that all sorts of research centers have located around Princeton, partly to be near the university and partly to be near each other, I guess. Uncle Al said maybe it's because they want to pick each other's brains, but again I don't know whether he was serious or not. I could understand the reason for most of the research places, but one sort of puzzled me. That was what Uncle Al said is called Public Opinion Research. It seems that a lot of people go around and ask a lot of other people questions on almost any subject. Then they write down the answers and publish the results. That seems sort of silly to me and I said so.

"Haven't you ever heard of the Gallup Poll?" Uncle Al asked.

"Yes," I replied. "They predict elections and things like that."

"Well, there are dozens of other polls like it, and they operate all year round. They're liable to ask what your opinion is on anything from the atom bomb to the weather."

38

"Well, when they go out and ask these questions, do they ask experts?" I asked.

"No, just the man on the street," Uncle Al answered.

"But he might not know what he was talking about."

"He probably doesn't."

"Well, I don't see the sense in that," I objected. "Why go ask a lot of people that don't know more about a subject than anyone else? Who cares what their opinion is? Isn't your own just as good?"

"You know, I never thought of it in that way before," Uncle Al said. "But you've got a point. Getting the opinion of a hundred thousand ignoramuses probably isn't half as important as finding out what one intelligent man thinks."

Uncle Al said that there were several independent firms that did research on order. In other words, if you were a big company and didn't have a research center of your own, you could take your problem to them and they would solve it for you. The more he talked, the more it seemed to me that this research business could be almost anything. If you could build up a big organization just by asking questions, why, there was nothing to it. My father's always claimed that I ask more questions than any ten people that he ever knew. While we were still riding around looking at the countryside I decided that research was the field for me.

Monday, June 24th

Well, I went into the research business today. It was simpler than I thought it would be. All it took was a can of paint and now I've got somebody who wants to be a partner and is willing to contribute something to the business. I haven't made any money yet, but even in the research business I imagine it takes a day or so to get rolling.

At breakfast this morning, I asked Uncle Al if it would be all right if I used the barn on the vacant lot down the road.

"Of course it will be all right," he said. "It's your barn—or rather it belongs to your mother."

After Uncle Al had gone to the office, I asked Aunt Mabel for a can of paint and a brush. She rummaged around down in the basement and found a good-sized can of white paint, which she gave to me without even asking what I wanted it for.

Uncle Al has one of those light-weight magnesium ladders in his garage, which I carried down to the lot. I set it up against the end of the barn facing the road, climbed up, and marked off some lines for my sign. I'm pretty good at most subjects in school but the thing I'm probably best at is art. My art teacher keeps telling me that I should be a professional artist when I grow up. If I decide not to be a naturalist, maybe I will be. As it is, maybe I'll draw bugs and birds and things like that. Anyhow, I like making things like signs, and I'm pretty good at it, if I do say it myself.

I measured off the lines very carefully and roughed in the letters of my sign with a carpenter's pencil. When I had everything spaced right, I began to paint. On the top line, in letters about two feet high, I put HENRY REED, INC. Then I moved down several feet, marked off two more lines, and penciled in the word RESEARCH. I got the paint and had started back up the ladder when a voice said, "What kind of research?"

I looked around, and there standing below me, with a butterfly net in her hand, was a little scrawny girl. She was wearing a pair of faded blue jeans, a blue and white checked shirt, and red sneakers. She had brown hair which was faded in spots from the sun and was drawn back in a sort of pony tail. She had a small face which was covered with freckles and light blue eyes that didn't miss a thing. She was nibbling on an apple like a little rabbit. If she hadn't had such a sharp-pointed nose, she would have looked like a rabbit too.

"Who are you?" I asked.

"Margaret Glass," she answered. "Everybody calls me Midge, and don't make any remarks about my being a little Glass, or that I'd better watch out or I'll get broken, because I've heard them all." She took another bite of the apple and then said, "Who are you?"

"That's me," I said, pointing to the sign up above my head.

"Henry Reed, Inc.," she said out loud. "You don't look incorporated." Then she went off into gales of laughter.

I saw right away that I had a crazy giggling girl to deal with. Her remark didn't make any sense at all, but she seemed to think it was funny. However, I didn't say anything because I had already figured out that she was the girl that my Aunt Mabel had mentioned. Since she was the only person near my age in town there was no use getting off on the wrong foot. My father, who is a pretty smart diplomat, says that if you have to get along with people, you might as well start right out in the beginning trying to like them. I was willing to try with this little apple-eater but it didn't look promising.

"How old are you?" I asked.

"Twelve," she replied.

I thought she was even younger than that because she was so small, but when you're twelve you're just a kid, not even in your teens, and that explains a lot. Kids that are not even in their teens are apt to be a little childish. I have been in my teens for more than a year, which makes a lot of difference.

"What kind of research you going to do?" she asked.

"Any kind of research that people want done," I replied.

"Pure or applied research?" she asked.

"What's the difference?"

"Well, in pure research you just sort of try and find out things because you're curious. In applied research you're trying to find the answer to some question. Is that clear?"

"Not very," I replied.

"All right, suppose I have a rabbit and I try feeding him a lot of different things just because I want to know what all a rabbit will eat. That's pure research. If somebody hires me to find out what the rabbits eat and will grow best on because he wants to sell rabbit food, that's applied research."

"I'm going to do both," I told her. "Pure research for myself, and applied research if somebody will pay me some money."

"That's sensible," Midge said. "You ought to put that in your sign."

44

"How does it happen you know so much about research?"

"My father's a research chemist." She finished her apple and threw the core over into the grass.

I was still up on the ladder. I drew the lines a little bit longer and started roughing out the letters to make the words PURE AND APPLIED RESEARCH. I worked for several minutes and Midge didn't say a word.

"I might join your firm," she said finally, "if you invited me nicely."

"Why should I?"

"Teamwork," she answered. "Teamwork's the thing these days in research. My father says things have gotten so complicated that one man alone can't discover much any more."

I thought this over for a minute while I kept working on my sign. If her father was a research chemist like she said, she probably knew quite a bit about how research organizations work, and also with the whole summer ahead of me I figured it might be nice to have someone to talk to, even if it was a girl a year and a half younger than I. I turned around and sat down on the ladder.

"What are you going to put into the business?" I asked. "I've got the property here, the building, a lot of pigeons which are inside, and one turtle." I waved my hand up at the half-finished sign, which was pretty good. "I'm even furnishing the sign."

"I'll furnish brains," she said.

Even though I always try to be polite, I laughed out loud at that, but she didn't seem to mind.

"Brains are the most important part of any research organization. My father says so."

"He's probably right," I admitted. "But the question is who has them? What grade are you in?"

"Seventh," she replied.

"There you are," I said. "I'm in the eighth grade so I've had more education. I've had more experience, too. I'm a teen-ager and you're only twelve."

"That's no advantage," she said. "Who are all these delinquent children you read about in the papers? Teen-agers—that's you. Me, I'm not a teen-ager so I must be a respectable, law-abiding citizen."

She started laughing like an idiot again. I don't know what about, since her remark didn't even make any sense. I climbed down the ladder and put my can of paint and brush on a box. I sharpened my pencil and started toward the ladder again.

"I could also contribute a pair of rabbits," she said. "We could raise rabbits, and they use a lot of rabbits in research to test serum and drugs and feeds and things like that."

I thought this over for a minute. I've never had any rabbits because we have never lived anyplace where there was room enough. "What kind of rabbits?" I asked.

46

"Checkered Giants," Midge replied. "They're great big white rabbits with black spots."

"That might not be a bad idea," I said, "to have a few rabbits."

"You could just make that 'Reed and Glass, Inc.,'" she said, pointing up at my sign.

I had just finished painting the words "Henry Reed" and I didn't care much for the idea of changing my sign before it was half finished. "Let's see the rabbits first," I suggested.

She led the way across the street to a big white frame house which sat well back from the road. We went around the house to the back, past a little sunken stone-walled garden, and through a hedge to a small barn that was used for a garage. Beside this sat a little portable wire pen. Attached to one end of the pen was a tiny wooden house with a tarpaper roof. Only one rabbit was in sight. It was out in the pen, nibbling away at part of a carrot.

"That's Mathilda," Midge said.

Mathilda was an enormous rabbit. There was a small wire gate on top of the pen. I opened this, reached in, and picked her up. She weighed at least seven or eight pounds and was as strong and wiry as a wildcat. The minute I lifted her off the ground she started kicking like a mule and about the third or fourth kick she made several deep scratches in my wrist. I let her drop back down in the pen. She seemed healthy, all right.

47

I leaned down and tried to look in the little house, but it was too dark inside to see anything.

"How do you get him to come out of the house?" I asked.

"Oh, Jedidiah is not in the house," Midge explained. "He's over by your barn."

"By my barn?"

"Yes, he got loose and I was trying to catch him. That's how I happened to be over there. Look, we can chase Mathilda into the house and slide that little door shut. Then you can detach the house from the pen and we can haul them over there on the wagon. We're going to keep everything at the research center, aren't we?"

"Just a minute, the agreement was for two rabbits," I said. "Not one."

"Well, I've got two rabbits. All we have to do is catch the other one."

"All right, when we catch the other one I'll paint your name on the barn," I said. "Until we do catch him, it's going to stay 'Henry Reed, Inc.'"

"Okay," Midge agreed. "It's a temporary partnership until we catch Jedidiah. But you have to help me catch him."

"It shouldn't be too difficult to catch a rabbit," I said.

"No, it shouldn't. All you have to be is smarter than the rabbit."

She thought that was funny and started laughing again,

but I didn't even smile. If one expects to be the head of a successful business he has to be dignified.

We got Midge's wagon and carted the pen over on the first trip and the house with the rabbit inside on the second. Then we went back for the two crocks that she used for food and water and for a big pail full of rabbit food that looked like little tiny dog biscuits. While Midge got the rabbit pen all set up I went back to the sign. I finished painting the words PURE AND APPLIED RESEARCH and then climbed down from the ladder.

"That looks pretty good," Midge said approvingly. "Are you going to say anything else?"

"Maybe later, when I figure out something to say. Now let's catch that other rabbit. Did you see where he went?"

"When I first came over here he was back there by that old lilac bush," Midge said, pointing. "He's probably still around there somewhere."

Agony had been trotting back and forth with us as we brought over the rabbit and the pen. He got sort of excited when he first saw the rabbit, but after he'd made about twenty-five circuits around the wire pen and saw that he couldn't possibly get in he gave up in disgust. However, since he was a rabbit dog I figured that he would probably take off if he saw a loose rabbit and chase it into the next county. I had his leash in my pocket, so I tied him up to the corner of the barn, which he didn't like

49

very much, and then Midge and I went over to the lilac bush.

We hunted for about five minutes and then I spotted the rabbit sitting calmly in a sort of half-nest in the tall grass, watching us and chewing away contentedly.

"Let me have the net," I said to Midge.

I sneaked around in back of the rabbit and crept up very quietly and slowly. Finally, just when I was within three feet of him, he gave a hop forward. I made a lunge and missed him by about three inches. That was bad enough, but the rabbit wasn't scared at all. He hopped off lazily toward the trees as if he wasn't really worried about our catching him.

"I almost had him," I said.

Midge shook her head. "He always lets you get within

50

a few inches of him. I think he likes to tease people."

"How long has this rabbit been loose?" I asked suspiciously.

"Oh, about six weeks," Midge replied.

"Six weeks!" I yelled. "Why he's practically a wild rabbit!"

"No, he isn't. Wild rabbits are brown."

"You know what I mean," I said disgustedly. "That's not very honest, buying your way into a firm with two rabbits one of which you can't catch."

"I probably could have caught him," Midge explained, "if it hadn't been for the Apples."

"What apples?" I asked.

"The sour Apples," Midge replied. "They're the people that live in that red brick house next door to your lot here. They're spiteful and ornery."

"What's that got to do with the rabbit?"

"Well, the rabbit has been over here most of the time since the day he got loose. There's a little brook at the back of your place and I suppose he gets water there. And of course there's plenty of grass and things to eat. I've been over here dozens of times trying to catch him, but every time I start chasing him he hops through the hedge onto the Apples' property. Mr. Apple won't let anyone put a foot on his land. He starts yelling and threatening the minute you even get near. Once I chased the rabbit all the way around his garage and he complained to my mother. He kicked up an awful fuss and so Mother has forbidden me to even go near their place."

"Why is he so ornery?" I asked.

"I don't know," Midge replied. "Maybe he's just naturally mean or maybe he's trying to hide something. I wouldn't be surprised if he had a whole lot of bodies buried over there. That would be a good research project —find out who he's murdered or what he's hiding."

"Let's get the rabbit first," I said.

We hunted until lunch time and we saw the rabbit only twice. I got near enough to try catching him with a net again and he did exactly the same thing. He made a lazy hop just in time to avoid being caught. I got more and more annoyed at that rabbit and Midge didn't help anything by saying that maybe the rabbit had more brains than our whole research organization.

After lunch I decided that maybe we were going at the whole thing wrong and that the right approach was to let Agony do what he was supposed to do—chase rabbits. Uncle Al came home for lunch and I asked him about it and he said that a well-trained beagle hound would chase a rabbit around in a circle so that the hunter could get a shot. I figured that if Agony would chase the rabbit around in circles I might get a chance to land him with the net as he went by. And if I didn't, in time he should get tired out. I figured that a big, fat tame rabbit shouldn't be able to run nearly as fast as a wild one.

I thought Midge might worry for fear Agony would catch the rabbit and kill it, but she didn't seem to mind. We started with Agony on a leash, working back and forth through the grass near where we had last seen Jedidiah. Agony seemed to enjoy his work and went sniffing around as happily as could be. We hadn't been hunting more than five minutes when he let out a bay that sounded like a woman yodeling. Uncle Al had said that when a beagle was after a rabbit he had a bay that beagle owners claimed was beautiful and musical, but that some people, himself included, thought it sounded like a woman being murdered. After I got over being surprised, I thought Agony had a beautiful voice, but Midge stuck her fingers in her ears.

Whether Agony's voice was beautiful or not, it certainly scared that rabbit. He didn't do any lazy hopping this time, but took off like a streak. Agony nearly choked himself to death trying to get away to chase him.

"He's headed straight for Mr. Apple's place," Midge said. "He knows he's safe there."

With Agony half pulling me, we followed the rabbit. With his nose to the ground, Agony sniffed along through the grass and leaves, straining and struggling to get away and go after Jedidiah. He led us through the edge of the woods and up to a tall privet hedge. The rabbit must have gone through this because Agony stood sniffing at it, anxious to go through after him.

When you stand up close to the hedge you can see through without any difficulty. The Apples' house is a great big red brick building that sits, cold and ugly, in the middle of a big green lawn.

"That is a French provincial château," Midge said. "I know because Mrs. Apple told my mother that it was. They're quite proud of it."

The house does look something like a French château. It has a steep, pitched slate roof and about six chimneys. "A lot of French châteaux are ugly," I said, "but I never saw one quite as ugly as that."

"Have you been to France?" Midge asked.

"Sure," I said. "France, Italy, England, Austria, Switzerland."

She looked at me round-eyed. I guess that made quite an impression. It's funny the things that will impress girls. I didn't tell her that I'd never been to Florida, or Maine, or even Philadelphia or a lot of places like that. There was no use going into details, and besides I thought we'd better stick to the subject, which was the white rabbit.

"Where do you suppose Jedidiah went?" I asked. "He's worse than the rabbit in *Alice in Wonderland*."

"Oh, he's over there someplace," she said. "He always is. You see that big hedge across the back of his lawn?"

A tall privet hedge separates Mr. Apple's lot from my mother's. There is another hedge on the opposite side of the Apples' lawn, and one running across behind the garage, joining the two.

"You mean the hedge at the back of his property?" I asked.

"That isn't the back of his property," she explained. "On the other side of that there's still more lawn. His place goes back almost as far as yours. Most of it's lawn. Mr. Apple spends a lot of time out there, watering it and raking it and taking care of it—much more time than he does on the lawn up here."

"Why?"

"I don't know," she replied. "He's always plowing up little patches of it with a tractor and then seeding it down again. I wasn't kidding when I said he might be burying bodies. There's lots of room back there."

"Oh, he's just a fuss-pot about his lawn," I said. "Anyhow, let's solve one mystery at a time. I'm going to turn Agony loose and see if he can find that rabbit."

"The Apples aren't going to like it if Agony trespasses on their ground."

"You mean he'd get sore if a dog walked across his grass?" I asked.

"They get sore if a shadow falls on their ground," she said. "I bet a nickel he shoots robins."

"I don't see anybody around," I said, unfastening the leash from Agony's collar.

Agony is a smart dog. He was off like a flash, sniffing

55

along the ground and turning this way and that. He tracked that rabbit out into the middle of the lawn, made a couple of circles, and disappeared under a spreading yew. A second later he gave voice, and if any rabbit within five miles didn't shake in his boots he must have been deaf. Then we saw a flash of white and the rabbit went streaking across the lawn in back of the Apples' house with Agony close behind, baying like mad. In a shorter time than it takes to write this they disappeared around the far corner of the house.

"He'll probably chase him around the house and back this way," I said. "Beagles are supposed to chase rabbits in circles."

"Let's move up toward the road," Midge suggested. "There's a hole up there in the hedge where Jedidiah usually goes through when I'm chasing him. He'll probably come back that way."

We ran along the hedge toward the road. Agony and the rabbit were still out of sight, but as we ran his baying changed and went a note higher and he seemed to be even more excited. Then the sound grew louder as he rounded the other corner of the house and came back in our direction. We reached the hole in the hedge that Midge had mentioned, and waited. Then we saw a white streak dodging back and forth among the shrubs on the Apples' lawn, heading generally in our direction. I could only half see either Agony or the rabbit because of the hedge. I waited beside the hole, but instead of coming through they went past, going so fast they were just white streaks. Agony was pounding along about three feet in the rear. How he could run so fast and bay so constantly I'll never know. Suddenly the white streak made a quick turn and doubled back the way it came, running close along the hedge on the other side. This time I took no chances. I stuck the net through the hole and as it went by—whammo!—I brought the net down on top of it.

Agony was going too fast to stop. He ran smack into the butterfly net, almost knocking it out of my hand. Then he did a double somersault and ended by sliding about three feet on his hind end. He got to his feet and came back, growling and sputtering.

The open end of the net was against the ground and I was afraid to turn it over for fear that the rabbit would get out. I pulled it back, sliding it along the ground until it was on our side of the hedge. The net is a homemade one. I guess it was made out of an old curtain. You can't really see through it, and all I could tell was that there was something white inside and I didn't know which end of the rabbit was which. I was decorated with a couple of deep scratches already from a rabbit and I didn't want any more.

"Go back and find me a board or something and I'll slide it over the open end of the net," I told Midge.

She ran off and a minute later came back with the top

of a peach basket. I laid this flat on the ground and slid the net on top of it. Then I picked up the top, holding the net down tightly around the edges, and carried the whole works back to the barn. Midge opened the top of the rabbit pen and I dumped in our prize. As I did it gave a terrible yowl.

"Holy Ned! It's Siegfried!" Midge shouted.

I looked and what we had caught was not a rabbit at all but a great big white tomcat. He was crouched in the center of the pen, trying to figure out what had happened. He glared at Mathilda, our other white rabbit, and his tail began swinging back and forth. That cat was in a rage and the rabbit was the nearest thing in sight.

"I'd better get him out of there," I said. "He might attack the rabbit."

"Don't go in after him," Midge warned. "That cat is a holy terror. Just open the door and let him out."

Agony hadn't figured out what had happened back by the hedge, and he had stayed behind, sniffing around the ground. I guess he finally got discouraged because at this point he came running up to the rabbit cage. He saw the cat inside and started to growl ferociously.

"If I let the cat out Agony's liable to kill him."

"That wouldn't be much loss," Midge said. "He's the meanest cat I've ever seen. He kills birds just for the fun of it."

I snapped Agony's leash back onto his collar and we

58

tied him to the corner of the barn again. Then we gave the cat a couple of pokes with a stick through the wire and he jumped out through the open door. Agony about went crazy trying to get at him, but I guess the cat knew that he was safe. He put his tail up in the air, spat a couple of times, hissed, and then walked off, very dignified, toward the Apples'.

"You're a fine hound," I told Agony. "You disappear around one corner of a house chasing a white rabbit and come around the other one chasing a white cat. I'm ashamed of you."

If Agony was ashamed he didn't show it. He jumped and barked and pulled and tried to get away to go after Siegfried.

"I wonder how Jedidiah did it?" Midge asked. "You know that rabbit's not only smarter than we are, he's smarter than Agony and he's smarter than Siegfried."

I didn't say anything. I was disgusted. Besides, before I had a chance to say anything, a state highway patrolman came driving along. He slammed on his brakes when he saw us, pulled over to one side of the road, and stopped.

"Do you know where some people by the name of Apple live?" he asked.

"The Apples reside in that French château," Midge replied, in a very lofty voice. "And if I were you, I'd have my gun handy. They're dangerous."

"Thanks, sis," said the patrolman and drove on.

59

"Bodies!" said Midge. "He does have bodies buried back there. Come on, let's hurry over and watch them dig them up."

"Bodies!" I snorted, but I went along.

When we got to the hedge Mrs. Apple and the trooper were standing on the side lawn facing the hedge. She was worked up about something and was waving her arms in excitement.

"This horrible hound actually came right on the property here and attacked my poor cat!" she said. "Poor Siegfried got away from this beast somehow and went running across the lawn. The thief must have trained his dog, because the dog deliberately chased him right over there by the hedge where this man caught him with a net. Seigfried is a very valuable cat and I want you to find him right away!"

"We'll do our best," the trooper said mildly.

"I just know this man kidnaped him to sell him someplace," Mrs. Apple said excitedly. "I read an article about it in a magazine. They steal valuable dogs and cats and then take them away to other cities and sell them."

Midge poked me in the back. "She doesn't mean kidnaping. She means catnaping," she said. Then she started slapping her leg and snorting and giggling as though she had said the funniest thing in the world.

"Hey, look," I said, pointing, "if you really want to see something funny." There was Siegfried. Where he had

60

been I don't know, but he was on his way through the hedge from our side. He came out on the other side and started across the lawn toward Mrs. Apple, his tail held high in the air, walking slowly and proudly as though he owned the place, which I guess he does.

The trooper saw the cat first. Probably Mrs. Apple was too excited to see anything. "Is that your cat coming over there?" he asked, nodding his head toward Siegfried.

Mrs. Apple saw the cat and let out a relieved yell. "Siegfried, darling, you got away!" she said. "You poor, poor cat."

The trooper had been holding a notebook which he now folded up and put away. "I'm glad your cat is back, Mrs. Apple," he said, touching his cap. "I'll be on my way now."

"I still want you to find the man who stole him," Mrs. Apple said. "I tell you I saw it with my own eyes."

"Yes, ma'am, we'll do our best," said the trooper. However, he didn't waste any time asking any more questions.

Several minutes later we were back at the barn and he drove up again.

"Would you two know anything about a white cat being kidnaped?" he asked pleasantly.

"You mean catnaped, don't you?" Midge asked, going off again into gales of laughter. She liked the joke even better than she did over by the hedge. I guess she thinks her jokes are like cheese. They improve with age. The trooper laughed, too, but I imagine he was just being polite.

"I don't think anybody around here would try to steal a cat except by mistake," I said.

"If you mean that big white cat of Mrs. Apple's, nobody would want him," Midge said. "They might shoot him, but steal him, never!"

"Uh-huh," said the trooper. "Well, anyhow, he's back now."

Tuesday, June 25th

Nothing much happened today. Midge and I cleaned out the front part of the barn. We found an old table to use for a desk and three or four chairs so that we could sit down. She washed the windows and I managed to get the big front doors open and aired out the place. Agony located another turtle and I made a small wire pen and put it and the turtle that I found Sunday into it.

It certainly pays to advertise. People are beginning to notice my sign. I saw a number of people driving by in cars who paused for a minute to read it. I think almost everyone in Grover's Corner has seen it. I'm sure that the Apples have. The reason I know is that Mr. Apple came over to see Uncle Al tonight.

I didn't know Mr. Apple when he came to the door. He's a funny little man with a round head that's much too big for his body. He's almost bald, but what hair he has, he allows to grow long and combs it across the top of his head and fools nobody except himself. He's very precise and definite about everything he does, and you can tell that he's just as pleased with himself as it's possible to be.

I answered the door. "Is Mr. Harris at home?" he asked.

I invited him in, which I wouldn't have, had I known who he was or what he wanted. Anyhow, he and my uncle sat down in the living room, and since they didn't ask me to leave, I didn't.

"What can I do for you, Mr. Apple?" my uncle asked. He was polite but he was in a hurry, I knew, because there was a good fight coming on television at nine o'clock and it was a quarter of nine then.

"You are the owner of the property adjacent to mine, are you not?" Mr. Apple asked.

"No, that belongs to my sister," Uncle Al replied. "Hank's father and mother. Hank, have you met Mr. Apple? Mr. Apple, this is my nephew, Henry Reed."

"How do you do," Mr. Apple said rather frostily. "Henry Reed. Is that your name painted on the barn on the property of which I speak?"

"If you mean Henry Reed, Inc., Pure and Applied Research, that's me," I answered.

"I see," said Mr. Apple with a cold smile. Then he turned away from me as though I were about two years old and said to my uncle, "I presume you are in charge of the property?"

"Well, in a way, yes," Uncle Al admitted. "Why?"

"Well, it concerns this question of research," Mr. Apple said. "As you know this area is zoned residential A. Now I believe that you will find upon examining the zoning regulations that all commercial uses are excluded from residential zone A, unless they were already in existence at the time the zoning law became effective."

"You may be right," admitted Uncle Al. "I suppose that sign misled you. My nephew here is quite a good artist. When I noticed that sign for the first time I was sort of startled myself. It looks like a professional job. I understand what you're worried about. You thought there might be some huge building going up on the lot. Well, you've got nothing to worry about."

"Then your nephew is not going to continue with his activities there?" Mr. Apple asked.

Uncle Al looked startled, sort of like a surprised St. Bernard dog. "As I explained, Mr. Apple, it's only my nephew, this young lad here."

"I fail to see how age enters into the question," Mr. Apple said very precisely. "Commercial activities are specifically prohibited. Whether the proprietor is young or old does not matter."

Uncle Al lowered his head and looked at Mr. Apple from under his shaggy eyebrows. "Do you seriously mean, Mr. Apple, that you would object to Hank here and that Glass girl conducting some sort of a little business on that vacant lot during the summer?"

"I most certainly would," Mr. Apple replied firmly. "Whether children conduct the business or not is sheer sentimentality. The question that's important is whether the law is or is not being broken."

65

"Hank, have you sold anything from that barn?" Uncle Al asked abruptly.

"No," I said.

"Has anyone paid you for any services that you have performed on that property?"

"Not yet."

Uncle Al turned back to Mr. Apple. "Mr. Apple, I suggest you wait until you're hurt before you holler. Good night."

Mr. Apple got up to leave. I opened the door for him so he wouldn't be delayed.

For a while I thought I'd be out of business before I got started. Uncle Al was mad. He stomped around the room, muttering to himself, forgetting the fight completely. Aunt Mabel came downstairs and he told her what had happened. She got quite indignant about it, too. Uncle Al poked through his desk and hunted around until finally he came up with a copy of the zoning law. He sat down in his easy chair and read different parts of this for almost half an hour. Finally he gave a throaty chuckle.

"All right, I think we've got him," he said. "It says here 'all other provisions notwithstanding' that a farmer has a right to sell the produce from his land and that he can put up whatever sign he deems necessary to sell it. Okay, that land was a farm years before Mr. Apple moved into the town. So you just change the nature of your business. Right beneath the sign you have, put 'Agricultural and

Biological Research Supplies.' Then you can list whatever you want to sell, your turtles, your pigeons, and your rabbits. They're all agricultural products and he can't do a thing."

"What if someone comes and wants me to perform some research for them?" I asked.

"Well, we'll cross that bridge when we get to it," Uncle Al replied. "Off hand, I'd say go ahead and take any job you can get. In the meantime, I'm going to write him a letter from the office tomorrow and point out that this agricultural supply business is perfectly legal."

Friday, June 28th

Business has been sort of slow all week. In fact, nothing happened since Mr. Apple's visit last Tuesday until today. Today I got a new product. I'm in the earthworm business now. So far it's been very profitable and quite interesting.

The way it happened was that the garden needed cultivating. There were quite a few weeds in between the rows and I suggested to Aunt Mabel that maybe I ought to get out the tractor and plow it. She agreed that the garden needed cultivating but said that Uncle Al would probably feel cheated when he got home.

"You go ahead, anyhow," she said. "Al will just have to share his tractor this summer, now that he's showed you how to use it."

I got the tractor out, figured out how to attach the cultivator on the back, and plowed the whole garden twice in less than an hour. The tractor works like a dream. Just as I was finishing, a man in a dark blue car stopped at the side of the road and walked over to the fence. "Are you turning up any worms?" he asked.

"Quite a few," I told him.

"How about selling me a couple of dozen?"

I looked at him closely and he looked perfectly normal. "You want to buy some worms?" I asked.

"Sure, haven't you ever heard of selling worms?"

"I've heard of selling snails and grasshoppers and rattle-snakes, but never worms," I said. "How do you cook them?"

"You don't cook them at all," he replied. "I'm going fishing. Look, I'd sooner pay you twenty-five cents a dozen, say, than dig them myself. First place, I live in an apartment and haven't any place to dig. Secondly, it's just too much bother. You might dig half an hour before you find the right spot. Sometimes you can't find any at all."

The garden was full of worms so I found a can, filled it with dirt, and picked up about two dozen large worms. He gave me fifty cents and drove off perfectly happy. I decided immediately to go into the earthworm business. I had already made the change in my sign that Uncle Al had suggested, except that I had listed just turtles and pigeons. There was no point in saying that I had rabbits to sell until I had more than one. Midge and I tried three different times during the week to catch that rabbit and each time he got away.

I went to the basement to get the can of white paint and a brush so that I could add earthworms to my sign.

On my way out of the house Aunt Mabel called to me from the kitchen.

"If you enjoy operating that little tractor, why don't you take the sickle bar and mow your lot?" she asked. "Al usually does it once or twice a year to keep the place from going completely to jungle."

I unhooked the cultivator and hooked the two-wheel cart on behind the tractor, put the sickle bar, paint, and brush in the cart, and drove off toward the lot. Agony as usual tagged along.

Midge appeared about ten seconds after I did, and immediately wanted to operate the tractor. She helped me hook up the sickle bar and I made a couple of turns around the lot, and cut a swath about three feet wide. Agony kept running ahead of the tractor so we had to tie him up. I was afraid I would cut off his legs.

I mowed for about half an hour and then turned the tractor over to Midge while I added EARTHWORMS to our sign. She finished mowing about the same time I finished painting. What with the whole end of the barn just about covered with the sign, and all the grass freshly cut, we looked pretty snappy.

"What are you going to keep the earthworms in?" she asked.

"Dirt," I replied.

"Yes, but you can't waste time going out and digging them every time someone wants to buy a few. Besides, when it gets dry they go down so deep you'll have to dig all day to get them."

"I know," I said. "What I need is something like a great big tub."

"I'll tell you something else we need," Midge announced. "A bale of straw for the rabbit's house. I cleaned it out this morning but I didn't have any straw to put in it."

"Where do you get straw?" I asked.

"At Mr. Baines's farm," Midge said. "You go past your uncle's house, and a little ways down the road there's a lane on the right. You turn down it and he lives way back in the field. Usually my father drives me down to get it but we could go down in the tractor and cart."

We detached the sickle bar and I took it home and put it in the garage. Aunt Mabel said it was all right to use the cart, so we drove off down the road. I drove the tractor, Midge sat on the seat in the little cart, and Agony sat in the cart itself. That dog would rather ride than do anything, even chase cats.

Mr. Baines's farm was a sprawling old place with a white house and about seven red barns. We had to hunt through all of them before we found him. We bought a bale of straw for fifty cents and put it in the cart and were about to leave when Midge spotted an old bathtub sitting beside a machinery shed.

"Are you going to use that bathtub, Mr. Baines?" she asked.

Mr. Baines was a tall, lanky man with a long, crooked nose. He looked at Midge and said, "I doubt it. I got it about six years ago. Somebody gave it to me. I was going to use it for a watering trough. Then I couldn't find the right fittings to close that hole in the bottom so I set it there. It's been there ever since."

"Do you want to get rid of it?" Midge asked.

"You can have it, but I don't know how you can get it home without a truck," Mr. Baines said. "I'll bet that weighs a good two hundred pounds."

"Don't you think it'll go in the cart?" I asked.

"It's too long for that little cart," he said. He scratched his neck and then said, "Tell you what. There's an old buggy in that machinery shed that I've been meaning to get rid of for some time. We'll load the bathtub into the buggy. You can hitch the buggy behind the cart and take the whole shebang."

He called his hired man and the three of us pulled and pushed and lifted, and finally we got the bathtub into the buggy. The buggy was really what you'd call a spring wagon, according to Mr. Baines, with one seat up front and quite a long body, so there was plenty of room for the tub. We found a piece of rope and tied the buggy on behind the cart. Since the cart was now filled with the bale of straw there wasn't any place for Agony. He wanted to ride,

so Midge picked him up and put him in the bathtub. That suited him fine. He stood up on his hind legs, put his front legs over the edge of the bathtub, and watched everything happily. Midge decided on the buggy, too, and climbed up and sat down in the seat.

It was a pretty heavy load for the tractor, and for a while I thought it wasn't going to pull it. The tractor has three gears, though. I managed to get started in low and slowly we picked up speed. By the time we'd gone halfway down the lane we were moving along at a fairly respectable clip. We reached the road and I was able to turn left onto the black-top without having to stop for traffic.

There's a ditch between my lot and the road and just one narrow spot where there's a driveway over a metal culvert. I knew I would have to hit this fairly square, so I swung way over to the opposite side of the road and then made a sharp turn so I could go in the driveway straight. The tractor was just about to the edge of the road, with the cart and buggy stretched out behind all the way to the opposite side, when Midge suddenly let out a yell and said, "Stop!" I jammed on the brake and killed the engine.

"What's the matter?" I asked.

"There's a turtle right ahead of you," she said, standing up and pointing. "You're going to run over it."

I got off the tractor and picked up the turtle. That made

three we have. A car was coming down the road and I decided I'd better get out of the way, so I climbed back on the tractor. I pulled the starter wire but the engine wouldn't start.

I don't know what I did. Uncle Al says I must have flooded the engine. Anyhow, I did something and it simply wouldn't start. The car that I'd seen drove up and stopped because it couldn't get by. Then one came from the other direction and it had to stop. I kept pulling on the wire, trying to start the tractor engine, but it wouldn't even cough. By this time there were six cars. Finally two of the men got out and came over and tried to help me. They both tried to start the engine and had no more luck than I had. Another five minutes went by and another five cars stacked up in both directions. It was a few minutes after five o'clock and people were on their way home from work. Ordinarily there isn't much traffic along that road, but of course this time there was. I was feeling sort of nervous and embarrassed about it all, but Midge didn't seem to mind. She still sat in the buggy, looking out over all the cars and waving to people she knew. Agony was in the bathtub, poking his head over the edge, and barking first from one side and then the other. A man with a big camera was in one of the cars and he came up and took three or four pictures.

About ten people tried to start the tractor but it wouldn't budge. Finally one man said, "Look, we're liable to be

75

here all night if we wait for mechanical power to get this rig off the road. Let's all take hold of it and we'll pull it off."

Several of them pushed the tractor, two or three got behind the buggy, and several pushed on the cart. I sat on the tractor and steered. With so many people it was no trick at all, and in a minute we had rolled off the road and onto the lot. The man with the camera was taking pictures as we went.

As the traffic jam cleared away I looked over at the entrance to Mr. Apple's place, and there stood Mr. and Mrs. Apple, glaring at everybody.

"They were hoping somebody would trespass on their lawn so they could snarl at them," said Midge.

We were well off the road, but I still wanted to get the bathtub over near the barn. I got off and gave one pull on the starter wire, and naturally the motor started immediately. I pulled the buggy over where I wanted to put the bathtub and then Midge and I tried to figure out how to get it down from the buggy without smashing everything, including our toes.

"What are you going to put in that bathtub?" a man asked.

We turned around and there was the man who had been taking all the pictures.

"Earthworms," I said, "if I can get it off this buggy."

He glanced at my sign on the end of the barn and then

said, "What are you going to do, give your earthworms a bath before you sell them?"

"No, I just want a place to keep them," I said. "I don't want to have to go digging up the entire lot every time someone wants a dozen."

"Well, I don't know why earthworms shouldn't be happy in a bathtub. Here, I'll give you a hand."

Together we slid the bathtub off the buggy and over against the side of the barn. Then he took a picture of my sign and asked a lot of questions. I told him all about why I started the research business, that I wanted to be able to report on an example of free enterprise to my class back in Naples. I also mentioned that I was having a little bit of trouble with one neighbor who was complaining that I had violated the zoning law. He seemed very sympathetic and wished both Midge and me success. He shook our hands and promised that he would buy all his earthworms from us.

Tuesday, July 2nd

Business has been pretty good since my last entry. I sold two pairs of pigeons to a man for a dollar a pair and I sold three dozen earthworms. Midge and I filled the bathtub with dirt and we must have several hundred earthworms in it by now. Everyone says it gets pretty dry late in July and we want to have a good supply on hand before it gets too hard to find them.

We haven't caught Jedidiah yet, although we've certainly tried. Midge has started to keep score on the side of the barn of how many times we've tried to catch him. It's up to thirteen now. She's really anxious to get her name up there on the end of the barn as a member of the firm, but I won't do it. I believe in sticking to an agreement. Business is business. Until we have two rabbits she is not a full member of the firm.

I think that the pictures and the article in the newspaper are the main reason why Midge is so anxious to have the firm name changed to Reed and Glass, Inc. The man who was taking the pictures last week, while we were getting our buggy and bathtub, turned out to be the editor of the *Princeton Bugle* and he had a story about the firm in the paper this week.

There was a good shot of the sign on the end of my barn. You could read every word of it. Underneath the picture it said, "New research organization locates at Grover's Corner." I figure that a picture on the front page is better than a lot of classified advertising saying that I have earthworms, pigeons, and so on.

There was also a picture of everybody pushing on the buggy and the cart and the tractor, showing all the cars stopped on the road. I don't see much point in putting that in the paper, and the caption he had underneath it didn't make any sense at all. It said, "Two professors, one assistant professor, two vice-presidents, and five assorted Ph.D.s tackle problem of horseless carriage."

There was an article about the trouble we had and about our research firm. It is pretty long so I'm going to paste it here in the journal to save copying it.

CRISIS SOLVED BY SOME OF
PRINCETON'S BEST BRAINS

There was a minor crisis last evening at Grover's Corner a few miles outside of Princeton. It seems that the new research firm of Henry Reed, Inc., was engaged in moving some heavy equipment to the site of their new research center at Grover's Corner. Mr. Reed, president of the firm, was driving a small garden tractor to which was attached a cart with a bale of straw and following that a buggy with the rather unlikely cargo of a bathtub. Mr. Reed was assisted by the vice-president of his firm, Miss Margaret Glass, who was superintending the operations from the seat in the buggy. Another member of the firm, a dog named Agony, was also present. He was riding in the bathtub. It is not known whether he was taking a bath at the time or not.

This entourage consisting of a tractor, a cart, and a buggy had just made a wide sweeping turn to swing into the research firm's grounds when the tractor stalled, effectively blocking the road in both directions.

Professor George Gore and Professor Justin Cartney, two of Princeton's outstanding engineers, endeavored to start the tractor. It refused to respond. Three members of Princeton's Aeronautical Engineering Department also tried their hand, without success. This prompts the *Princeton Bugle* to observe that although Princeton scientists have designed engines capable of producing several thousands of horsepower and have probed deeply into the secrets of the atom, they have yet to solve the problem of how to make a gasoline lawnmower or similar small engines operate properly.

The impasse of the stalled tractor was finally solved by team-work. Several New York advertising executives, a psychologist, a professor of sixteenth-century German literature, and the aforementioned engineers all joined hands to push the tractor and buggy clear of the road.

The traffic jam was soon cleared, but your reporter stayed a few moments to interview Mr. Reed and Miss Glass as to the nature of their research enterprise. Mr. Reed explained that one of the primary objectives of his organization is to demon-strate how free enterprise functions. He is returning to Naples, Italy, this fall where his father is a consul in the U.S. diplomatic service. He wishes to report at first hand on examples of free enterprise in the United States today. Miss Glass, when questioned as to why she had entered the research business, was quite brief and to the point. "Money," she said, "and you can quote me."

The firm of Henry Reed, Inc., operates in a very straight-forward manner. We feel that it is an excellent example of free enterprise. It takes objects which are ordinarily considered free and with a little enterprise sells them. Earthworms are an excellent example. Fishermen will be glad to know that earth-worms can be purchased at any time from Henry Reed, Inc., at twenty-five cents a dozen. The worms may be used for either research or fishing. Other products include pigeons, turtles, and rabbits.

The Princeton community welcomes Henry Reed, Inc., and wishes it every success. It is felt that a firm of this type has long been needed and certainly if it can call upon the assistance and talent which it mustered last Friday, it should go far, even with a balky engine.

As anyone can see, the article was a little inaccurate in places, but it was good publicity. Uncle Al had picked up the paper during the day and first thing when he came in the house for dinner he showed it to Aunt Mabel. She read it and laughed until tears came to her eyes. "That's quite amusing," she said finally, "isn't it?"

Uncle Al chuckled. "Yes, it is," he said. "And it also proves a point." He turned to me. "Say, did your mother ever tell you what her nickname was when she was a kid?"

"I don't think so."

"Well, everybody here in Grover's Corner called her the Turmoil Kid."

"Why?"

"Well, it would be easier to give you an illustration than to explain," he said. "When you get back home just call her that, and see what she says." He started filling his pipe. All of a sudden he stopped and stared off into space.

"What is it?" asked Aunt Mabel.

"I just figured out why our foreign relations are in such a stew," he said.

"Come on, both of you get out of the kitchen and get washed up for dinner," Aunt Mabel said in a very stern voice.

We were having our dessert when Uncle Al looked over at me and said, "I noticed your ad in the paper about the beagle. Has anyone called about him?"

"No."

82

"Sort of surprising, isn't it?" he asked.

"Yes, it is," I agreed. "I described him pretty accurately, I thought."

"There's no question about that," Uncle Al said.

I was still thinking about my mother's nickname. It will be a lot of fun if I have a few stories about her that I can sort of hold over her head when I get back home this fall. "How about giving me that illustration of why my mother was called the Turmoil Kid?" I asked.

"Well, the details have become confused over the years," Uncle Al said. "As a matter of fact I think the details were usually confusing to everyone except Jane at the time. I never figured out how things happened."

"What are some of the things that happened?" I insisted.

"Well, I'll just give you a very mild example," he said. "This was one of the late ones. Your mother was about seventeen, I guess. I'm nine years older than she is, so that would have made me about twenty-six. It was summertime and your mother had a date to go over to a play at New Hope, at the Bucks County Theater there. I don't know what happened to the boy friend. Maybe he broke a leg or had the measles or something. Anyhow, she had the two tickets and no one to take her. Foolishly, I let her persuade me to go. The folks were away and so we decided to go over and eat dinner and then go to the theater. To begin with we'd gone about four miles when we had a flat tire."

83

"Well, that was certainly nobody's fault," Aunt Mabel said.

"I admit that. It was no one's fault," Uncle Al agreed. "Very few things that happened when Jane was around were her fault. I don't dispute that, but the point is that they always happened. If she had not been along, I would not have had a flat tire.

"Anyhow the flat tire was fixed and we got rolling again," Uncle Al went on. "Well, when we got to New Hope the bridge was being repaired so we had to drive four or five miles up the Delaware River to find a bridge and then come back." Uncle Al paused and grinned. "Nothing much happened at dinner. I ordered some clam chowder and Jane had to put her purse on the floor where the waiter could trip over it and he spilled at least half a bowl down my right sleeve." Uncle Al held up his hand and looked at Aunt Mabel. "The man was a clumsy waiter. I admit it," he said.

"In spite of all these things we got to the playhouse early. We strolled around back where there was a great big maple. The first thing Jane did was to notice a little bird clinging to a twig. About three feet above it was a nest. She went on and on about this bird having fallen out of the nest, and how sooner or later it was going to fall from this branch and dash its brains out on the ground below. They'd been painting the back of the playhouse and there was a ladder still standing against one of the

84

walls. Finally, to shut her up, I moved the ladder over against the limb and climbed up to save the baby bird. The ladder didn't reach quite far enough, or rather it wasn't out quite far enough. I had to get off of it, and edge onto the limb out to the bird. Meanwhile, Jane saw some people she knew and went off with them to have a Coke. I got the bird back in its nest but when I started to get back onto the ladder, it slipped and went over against the trunk of the tree and there I was stranded. I had to yell and holler for someone to help me. Pretty soon there were about a hundred people down there giving me advice, laughing, and watching me climb down. I felt silly as could be, and of course Jane, being only seventeen and a girl, decided that it was all very embarrassing. She pretended she didn't know me at all."

Uncle Al paused and lighted his pipe. I expected him to go on and say something more but he didn't. Finally I asked, "Is that all of it?"

"That's all of it," he said. "That's the end of the story. We saw the play and came back home."

I didn't get the point and I told him so. "You mean nothing else happened?" I asked.

"That's all that happened," he said. He gave a sort of shiver as though he were cold.

Wednesday, July 3rd

Almost a week has gone by now and no one has called about my advertisement about Agony. I'm keeping my fingers crossed that no one ever will.

I sold another dozen earthworms today and we rigged up a trap to catch the white rabbit. We haven't had a chance to try it out yet, but I think it will work. I found a roll of fine mesh wire about seventy-five feet long. We put this in a big semicircle around the lilac bush where the rabbit often sits. We left a big, wide opening toward the trees and we scattered some rabbit food beside the lilac bush. Maybe the rabbit will hop in and we'll catch him there and block the opening. If he doesn't do that, maybe we can drive him in.

Before we set up the fence Agony saw the rabbit and took out after him. The rabbit went down a hole back in the woods. Agony started digging but it looked to me like the hole went back a long way underneath the roots of a big cottonwood. However, Agony wanted to dig so we left him there. About an hour later we decided to go back and see how he was doing. We found the hole but Agony wasn't there any longer. We were near the edge of the back part of Mr. Apple's place so we went over to the hedge to peek through. We were quite a distance from the road, and when we got to the hedge we were opposite the big square back lawn that Midge had mentioned. There was a tall hedge on all four sides and the whole area was nothing but grass. A lot of stakes had been driven here and there for no reason at all that I could see. And right in the center of the lawn there was a string tied around four stakes encircling a plot about twenty feet wide and forty feet long. In the center of this was Agony, digging a deep hole.

"Boy, will Apple blow his top when he sees that!" Midge said. "You better call him out of there."

I called and whistled but Agony didn't pay any attention. I couldn't call too loud because I was afraid Apple might be somewhere around and would hear me. I might just as well have shouted at the top of my voice, though, because a minute later he came through the opening of the hedge from the front part of the lot and saw Agony.

I've never seen a man so mad. His face got red and he jumped up and down and shouted and screamed. He looked around for something to throw but his lawn was so neat there wasn't a thing. Finally he took off his hat and threw it on the ground. Then he disappeared through the hedge again and was gone about a minute. When he came back he was running and carrying a pitchfork.

"Get off my grass, you filthy hound," he screamed.

"Here, Agony," I called. I don't know whether Apple heard me or not but I didn't care.

Agony stopped digging. I don't think he heard me but he did hear Mr. Apple. He looked up sort of curious-like, his nose all covered with fresh dirt. With his head cocked to one side, he stood watching Mr. Apple. He didn't seem frightened at all.

Apple was in such a rage that I doubt if he even saw the string that was stretched around the stakes. It was a heavy cord and must have been strong, and the stakes must have been driven in quite deep. He tripped over it and went head over heels, landing flat on his face. The pitchfork went flying through the air. Agony decided that he'd seen enough and he went kiting toward the woods. He disappeared through the hedge up near the corner

toward the big lawn. Midge and I decided that we would be smart if we got out of there, too. By the time we got back to the barn, Agony was lying down on the old burlap bag just outside the door where he usually sleeps. He opened one eye and looked at us sort of lazy-like.

"What do you suppose Agony was trying to dig up?" Midge asked.

"I think he was just digging for the fun of it."

"No, he wasn't," Midge said. "He's got a real sharp nose. He smells something buried there."

"A bone," I said.

"Maybe lots of bones. Maybe a body."

"Don't be silly," I told her. "It's against zoning laws to bury bodies except in the cemetery, and Mr. Apple believes in obeying the law."

I thought it was a pretty funny remark but Midge said, "You're a riot," and made a sour face.

She persuaded me we ought to go back and see what Apple was doing. By the time we got there and had found a good spot where we could look through the hedge, Mr. Apple had pretty well filled up the hole that Agony had made. He packed the dirt down and very carefully scratched the surface. Then he disappeared for a few minutes and came back with a small bag and sprinkled what I suppose was grass seed on the bare spot. Then he roughed up the surface a little bit and patted it down again, doing all the work on his knees and very, very

89

carefully. When he finished he connected up a hose and sprinkled the whole patch with water. After finishing his work with the bare spot he was very careful not to step on the lawn enclosed by the cord. Instead he circled around and around, making certain that every bit of the area was well sprinkled.

"Now, what do you think?" Midge asked. "Isn't there something mysterious about the way he acts?"

"There's something mysterious about it," I said. "But I think the answer is that he's just a lunatic."

Thursday, July 4th

It is rather late but I think I will put down the day's events before I go to bed. This entry hasn't anything to do with private enterprise. It's simply about Independence Day. Since some of my class in Naples haven't been back in the United States for several years, I want to tell them about the Fourth of July and how it's celebrated. They may have a lot of wrong ideas just as I had.

All my life I've listened to my mother and father tell about how they celebrated the Fourth. They shot off firecrackers, threw torpedoes, shot roman candles, set off pinwheels and skyrockets, and stepped on red devils that cracked and popped. They made a racket all day long, burned their fingers, ate until they were sick, and had a wonderful, noisy time. No more. There aren't any fireworks. They're against the law in most states and New Jersey is one of them. Now you go sit in a big football stadium and watch someone else set off pinwheels and skyrockets. All the kids do now is fidget around on the hard cement seats and wait for the "boom."

Of course having the fireworks shot off for you is better than not having any at all. Uncle Al says that outlawing fireworks was a good thing because every year a number of people, usually children, got badly burned. Some were maimed for life and some were killed.

"Of course, now that we've made the glorious Fourth safe by banning fireworks," he said, "people take to the highways in droves and kill each other with their automobiles. I suppose I should take you down to the shore today but frankly I'm afraid to. I wouldn't drive anywhere for all the tea in China."

Aunt Mabel suggested that we go in for the fireworks at Palmer Stadium later and Uncle Al agreed. Since we can get to Princeton by the back roads, he was willing to drive that far.

Naturally I was disappointed about not having the kind of a Fourth my parents had told me about, but there was no use feeling sad about it. I decided to spend the day as I would a quiet Sunday, so I got a book and started to read. I was on the couch on the front porch and Uncle Al was puttering around some bushes beside the porch when a blue and white sedan exactly like Uncle Al's drove into the lane. Uncle Al looked around in annoyance and muttered something about visitors.

"It's Mr. Apple," I said in a low voice. "And he has a car exactly like yours."

"I know he has," Uncle Al said. "It doesn't make me like my car any better. However, I think he got his first so I shouldn't kick."

Mr. Apple got out of his car and marched across the

lawn like a small boy on his way to speak a piece in Sunday School. "Mr. Harris, I'm sorry but I have a complaint to make," he said. He didn't look a bit sorry.

"Yes, what's that?"

"That hound of your nephew's insists on coming over on my property and causing damage."

"What kind of damage?" Uncle Al asked, straightening up with a grunt.

"Well, he digs," Mr. Apple said. "Right in the center of my lawn."

Uncle Al looked at me with a question in his eyes. I nodded. "I saw him digging there once," I admitted. "I didn't know he had any other times."

"He is constantly running across my property," Mr. Apple said. "My wife has a cat and he frightens that. I don't think it's a bit too much to ask that he be kept on a leash."

"Keeping a dog on a leash out here in what is practically country is pretty tough on a dog," Uncle Al said. "Suppose I have Hank keep a closer eye on him. Then if he continues to bother you I guess we'll have to tie him up."

"I'm not interested in promises," Mr. Apple said.

Agony is a smart dog and I always will think he heard what was being said, and knew that he had to do something if he wanted to keep his liberty. He must have been hiding around the corner. Also, Siegfried gave him wonderful cooperation. There was a small squeak from the

93

big beech tree near the right side of the front lawn. I heard it but I wouldn't have thought anything about it if Agony hadn't appeared suddenly. He ran over to the bottom of the tree and started barking. I got up to investigate, and there was Siegfried up on a big limb with a half-grown bird in his mouth. His tail was switching back and forth as usual.

"Your cat is up in this tree, Mr. Apple," I called. "He's just killed a bird."

Uncle Al came over to stand beneath the tree. Mr. Apple came along too, but not very willingly.

"These animals do cause trouble," Uncle Al said agreeably. "Mabel would blow a gasket if she saw that cat up there with that dead bird. I suggest we give both the dog and cat another chance before we ask that they be tied up."

Mr. Apple got in his car and drove off, but I could see that he wasn't happy. He doesn't like Agony, and what happened this evening hasn't helped matters. And Agony doesn't like Mr. Apple.

Aunt Mabel invited Midge to go to Princeton with us to see the fireworks. We left here a short while after dinner. It was still light and naturally I should have seen Agony get in the car but I was busy talking to Midge. Agony does his best to go along in the car whenever he can. Sometimes I think he is able to make himself invisible until the car is a mile or two from home.

"All right, he'll have a nice long wait in the car," Uncle Al said. "And he'll probably be scared out of his wits by the fireworks. If he has any."

When we got to Palmer Stadium, there were hundreds of people there. We were directed to a big field by the stadium where there were row after row of cars. Uncle Al parked, and we all got out. We had walked half of the way to the stadium before I noticed Agony trotting along beside me.

"I've got to take this crazy dog back," I said. "I'll catch up with you."

"Are you sure you can find the car in all this mess?" Uncle Al asked.

"I think I'll take this sweater back, too," Aunt Mabel said. "I'll go back with him. You two go on and get the tickets. We'll meet you at the gate."

We threaded our way back through the cars until we came to a blue and white sedan. "Here it is," Aunt Mabel said.

I opened the door and Agony hopped in the back seat. Aunt Mabel hooked her sweater over the rope on the back of the front seat and said, "I suppose it would be best to lock it. We wouldn't want to lose either the dog or my sweater."

You can lock Uncle Al's car by pressing down the little buttons on the doors. Those on the front doors will pop right up again if you close the door afterward. That's to keep you from locking the door with the keys inside. However, you can close the front doors, push down the buttons from the back, and then close the back doors. The buttons on the back doors don't pop up again. Aunt Mabel locked her side of the car that way and I was about to do the same when I noticed the keys in the ignition. Uncle Al is always complaining about Aunt Mabel leaving her keys in the car and I knew she would never let him forget having done it himself in a place like that. I didn't say a word. I simply reached over, took the keys out of the ignition, and stuck them in my pocket.

The fireworks were wonderful even though I didn't get to shoot any off myself. The American Legion puts on the show and they did a good job. It doesn't start until it is dark enough for everything to show up well, so it was quite dark by the time it was all over.

We took our time leaving the stadium because we knew there would be a terrible traffic jam in the field. Most of the cars had gone by the time we headed for our car, although they hadn't gone far. There were a lot of cars at the far end of the field and more in the street. We strolled along until we were about in the middle of the field, and then Uncle Al looked around and said, "Well, where are we now?"

We all saw two blue and white sedans at about the same time. Beside the one nearest the stadium stood Mr. and Mrs. Apple. "Well, now, I wouldn't have thought the

Apples capable of such patriotism," Uncle Al said. "Or childish enough to be interested in fireworks. I'm surprised."

I wasn't surprised, because there had been more adults than children in the stands.

I would have walked past without saying anything, but Aunt Mabel believes in being neighborly. "Good evening, Mrs. Apple, Mr. Apple," she said as we passed behind the car.

Mr. Apple didn't reply. He looked at Uncle Al and said, "I'd like to know the meaning of this, Mr. Harris. That vicious hound of yours is in my car. He growls every time I get near the door."

Uncle Al looked flabbergasted for a minute and then he sighed. "I guess a mistake has been made," he said heavily. "Get Agony out of Mr. Apple's car, Hank."

I wasn't certain what had happened as I walked over to the car. I tried the handle of the car and of course it was locked. I forgot all about the keys in my pocket. Instead I turned to Mr. Apple and said, "You'll have to unlock it."

"I didn't lock it in the first place," he said peevishly, reaching in his pocket. His leaving his keys in the ignition must have been very unusual because he was dumfounded when he couldn't find them in his pocket. "I must have lost them," he said in a peculiar voice. "Agnes, look in your purse and see if you have your set."

She didn't, and still I didn't think about the keys I had taken out of the ignition. I glanced inside the car and saw

97

Aunt Mabel's sweater. Agony had knocked it down on the floor but it was there.

"I guess we'll have to get a garage man," Uncle Al said. "Since we are at least partly responsible for this predicament, I'll go get someone." He started toward our car and then looked at the traffic-jammed street. "It'll be quicker if I walk to a telephone somewhere."

"I'll see if one of these officers can suggest something," Apple said frostily.

Uncle Al started back toward the stadium and Mr. Apple toward a parked police car. Mrs. Apple hesitated a minute and then decided she preferred her husband's company to ours.

"Heavens, but I have caused a mess," Aunt Mabel said, putting her hands up to her face. "I picked the car, so it's all my fault. Also I suggested that we lock it."

When she said that about locking the car, I remembered the keys. I pulled them out of my pocket and held them out. "I know where the keys are," I said.

I unlocked the car and Agony jumped out. I got Aunt Mabel's sweater and then I pulled up all the buttons so that none of the doors were locked. I stuck the keys back in the ignition. Aunt Mabel watched me thoughtfully.

"If you drove our car around to this side so that it would be nearest the stadium, no one would ever know what really did happen," I said.

"That certainly isn't honest, but it seems like the most

sensible way of settling the whole matter," Aunt Mabel said, with a twinkle in her eye.

We were all sitting in the car waiting when the Apples returned. Uncle Al arrived at about the same time. "It's all been a perfectly understandable mistake," Aunt Mabel said pleasantly. "Mr. Apple thought our car was his. You see, I locked this when I brought my sweater back."

Mr. Apple looked from our car to his, a short distance away. He appeared doubtful. "Where are my keys?" he demanded.

"If that is your car over there, Hank says they are in the ignition," Aunt Mabel said. "Al is always scolding me for doing that, and I'm so relieved to know that I'm not the only one who does."

Mr. Apple walked off to look at the other car. He saw the keys in the ignition but still he looked uncertain. Mrs. Apple said something to him and he came back toward us. "I guess you're right," he called, "My apologies."

"Think nothing of it," Aunt Mabel said very sweetly.

Uncle Al drove by the garage he had telephoned, and told them not to bother. Then we started home. He was quiet most of the way.

"If I had had my wits about me, I would have noticed the license numbers," he said. "There has to be some explanation of all this or else you people are magicians. What I want to know is how you got this car unlocked if you locked it. I have the keys."

99

Tuesday, July 9th

Yesterday the firm of Henry Reed, Inc., started a new research project. I guess you would call this pure research because we're doing it mainly to satisfy our curiosity. I've learned one thing already about pure research. It isn't all just sitting around thinking. You can get some big blisters on your hands and I've got them.

I was cutting the lawn with the tractor about eleven o'clock when Midge appeared. She said that there was a new house going to be built up beyond the McMurtys', and that they had already started work digging the basement. McMurtys' is the last house on Midge's side of the road. She was all excited about it and wanted to go up and watch. Everybody likes to watch a new building going up, and in Grover's Corner a new house was a big event since there were only nine houses to begin with and another one meant more than a ten-per-cent increase. I finished what little lawn I had left to do and together we walked up the road to watch.

There weren't any carpenters there yet. Before a building goes up it always seems to have to go down first. This

100

was in the down stage. A bulldozer was digging a deep hole where the basement was to be, and near the edge of this was a truck with a peculiar tall derrick on the back of it. Two men were working away with it, rigging up something.

"What's that contraption?" I asked.

"He's going to drill a well," Midge replied.

I had never seen a well drilled before and it was very interesting. I stayed there watching until lunch time and right after lunch I went back again.

The drilling bit is a big, heavy piece of steel about eight feet long and about six inches in diameter. This is tied to a cable, which goes over a pulley at the top of the derrick. An engine on the back of the drilling truck pulls on the cable so that the bit rises about two feet, and then it is dropped suddenly. The bit goes thump, thump, thump, against the ground and pounds a hole deeper and deeper. By noontime the bit was down about twenty feet and had hit some rock. The man who was in charge didn't seem to mind. He just kept right on drilling. He says that the drill goes a little bit slower but that it goes right through rock without any trouble.

Two men set up the drilling rig but after it was operating smoothly one of them left. The man who stayed was an old man with wispy white hair and pants that were much too big for him. If it hadn't been for a pair of suspenders I'm sure they would have fallen off. There wasn't really very much for him to do, since the rig operated automatically. He stood around with both hands on his suspenders, now and then looking at the cable that was going up and down. Once in a while he went over to the rig and made some sort of adjustment. Part of the time he spent leaning against a big tree with his eyes closed. When I asked him about it he said sometimes he could tell better what was happening by the sound of and the feel of things than he could by watching. It was easy to see how this could be so, because every time that bit dropped, the ground shook all over Grover's Corner.

"How do you know where to drill so that you'll get water?" I asked.

"You don't," he replied. "Usually we just pick a spot that's fairly handy to the house so we can put the well pump in the basement. Most of the time around here we hit water sooner or later."

"That doesn't seem like a very scientific way of doing it," I said.

Mr. Marble—that was his name as I found out later—agreed that this wasn't very scientific. "That's a problem that no scientist has been able to solve, young fellow, and if you solve it you could make yourself a pot of money." He stopped and blew his nose and then said, "Of course, there's a lot of people who aren't so scientific who claim they *have* solved it."

"What do you mean?"

102

"Dousers," he said. "They claim they can locate water under the ground with a stick."

Midge and I were both interested and we asked a lot of questions. According to Mr. Marble, a douser uses a piece of fruitwood—apple, cherry, peach, pear, or whatever he likes best. He cuts off a small limb where there is a fork or crotch, just as you do when you make a slingshot. However, he uses a bigger piece of wood than you do for a slingshot. Both of the branches of the crotch are left about a foot long. Some dousers like to cut their dousing sticks when the sap is going up and some when the sap is going down. Mr. Marble says that the only sap that matters in his opinion is the sap that cuts the stick. From the way Midge laughed you would have thought that Mr. Marble was Bob Hope. I laughed a little myself to be polite, but I agree with my mother who says that puns are not only the lowest form of humor but she doubts if they're humor at all.

A douser takes hold of the two branches of the Y of his fruit stick, and holds it so that what would be the handle of the bean-shooter points straight up. He holds onto the stick very tightly and then walks around over the ground where he would like to drill a well. When he comes to a spot where there's water he's supposed to feel a pull on the stick. When the pull becomes very strong it will swing the stick completely around in his hands until the bottom of the Y points straight down.

"Does it work?" I asked Mr. Marble.

He nodded. "I've drilled a lot of wells where people have called in dousers to pick the spot and I've got some very good wells. On the other hand, I've got some good wells where I've picked the spot by spitting."

"How do you pick the spot by spitting?"

"Well, you just spit someplace and then drill where you spit. However I don't claim as much for that method as the dousers do for theirs."

"Did you ever douse a well?" Midge asked.

Mr. Marble shook his head. "No, but I've tried walking around with a stick. I couldn't feel a thing. The dousers claim that you either have it or you don't have it. I guess I don't have it."

"Do you think they really do feel anything pulling on the stick?" I asked.

"I think so," Mr. Marble admitted. "I've seen dousers hold a fresh stick so tight that when it twisted down it pulled the bark right off the wood where they were holding it. I watched them closely and I don't see how they possibly could have twisted that bark off as a trick. They held their hands steady and suddenly that stick twisted and pointed down."

"There ought to be some explanation," I said.

"There ought to be but there isn't," Mr. Marble said. "One time I drilled a well for a geology professor who lived up toward Clinton. He said that dousing was all a lot of nonsense and he was out to prove it. So he called in a douser, who picked a spot, and then this professor picked a spot based on what he knew about the rock strata and things like that. A man has to be pretty interested in an idea to pay for an extra well just to prove his point, but that's what this professor did. First, we drilled on his spot and we got hardly more than a trickle out of it, even though we went down a hundred and fifty feet. Then we went over to where the douser had told us to drill and we got about twenty gallons a minute at sixty feet."

"What'd the professor say?" Midge asked.

"He was flabbergasted," Marble replied. "He had this douser pick some other spots, but of course he couldn't afford to drill wells on all of them. Then he tried putting a rubber mat over a spot that the man picked and asked him to walk over it again. He had some sort of theory about current flowing up through the ground to the man's body but the rubber mat didn't make any difference. He finally gave up, and as far as I know no one has ever proved whether dousing does or doesn't work."

Midge and I decided that dousing would make a good research project. We cut four dousing sticks, one from an apple tree, two from a wild cherry, and one from an old quince tree that was at the back of my lot. We went back to where Mr. Marble was drilling the well and he showed us how a douser held the stick. I walked all around the lot but I couldn't feel a thing. Midge chose the quince dousing stick because she likes quince jelly. I don't know if that had anything to do with it or not but she had better luck. When she walked near a spot at about ten feet from where Marble was drilling the stick began to wiggle back and forth. She kept on for another five feet or so and it dipped straight down.

"I've got it! I've got it! I'm a douser!" she yelled.

I thought she was just playing a trick and I'm still not certain. Marble was quite interested.

"That's just the way that stick behaves with all of them," he said.

We tried all sorts of things with Midge. I put a blindfold over her eyes and turned her around two or three times so that she couldn't be certain of where she was going. Then I led her around, holding on to her so that she wouldn't fall into the hole that was being dug for the basement. The stick pointed down at the same spot every time. Whether there was any water there or not I'll never know, but according to the dousing rules there should be.

"I'm not fooling you. I actually can feel something pulling the stick down," Midge claimed.

We finally got tired of watching the well-drilling rig and the bulldozer, so we went back to our lot where it was a little quieter. Midge was quite pleased to discover that she was a douser. She took her stick and walked around the lot, trying to locate water. Finally she picked a spot about seventy-five feet from the barn.

"There's water here," she announced. "There's an even stronger pull here than there was back there where they're building the house."

Again I tried blindfolding her and each time she picked a spot within three or four feet of where she was before. I tried holding on to her hand, making certain that she didn't twist the stick just to fool me, but she claimed that destroyed the vibrations and she couldn't feel anything.

"You just haven't got it," she said. "It's a gift, just like a beautiful voice or curly hair."

"Or brains," I said.

That night at dinner I was telling Uncle Al about it and he said that a lot of people, scientists as well as well drillers, believed in dousing. Kenneth Roberts wrote a book about a man up in Maine who was famous for his dousing ability.

"I've heard a lot of people talk about dousing," Uncle Al said, "and all sorts of explanations. Old John Santos, who used to work for my father, was a douser. He claimed that he could find water if it wasn't deeper than about seventy-five feet and that the closer the vein of water was to the surface the stronger the pull. To his way of thinking, that explained why he couldn't douse for an oil well. Usually oil is much much deeper than that."

This morning Midge tried her dousing rod again and she said that there was an extra-strong pull at the spot that she had picked near the barn. If Uncle Al's friend was right, that means there should be water close to the surface. Anyhow, we decided to find out and we are drilling a well. I found an old buggy axle in the barn which is fairly heavy, and I borrowed a clothesline from Aunt Mabel. The spot that Midge picked is right beneath a big maple limb, so I got the ladder and we tied a pulley to the limb. I dug a hole about two feet deep with a post-hole digger and then we started drilling. We pull the buggy axle up and let it drop down. It kept wiggling all over, so finally I found a big piece of pipe back of Uncle Al's garage. It's about three inches in diameter and about three feet long. I set this up and let the axle go up and down inside that as a guide. We pour a little water down this pipe, raise the axle in the air, and then let it fall. Pulling on that rope was easy at first, since the axle only weighs about fifty pounds, but after you raise it about fifty times it begins to get awfully heavy. That's how I got blisters on my hands. We didn't get down very far today, since it took most of the day to set up our rig. We have rope enough to go down about twenty-five or thirty feet. If we haven't hit water by that time, then dousing is a lot of hooey as far as I'm concerned.

Wednesday, July 10th

Midge and I are rich! Nobody will believe us but it's true. People laughed at Columbus and Robert Fulton and Eli Whitney. They didn't care. They knew they were right. I know we're right, too, and before long we'll be famous as well as wealthy.

I went in to Princeton with Aunt Mabel so I didn't start drilling the well again until after lunch. Then Midge and I drilled for almost two hours. At first the drill went down fairly steadily and the end of the axle disappeared out of sight in the guide pipe. Then we hit something very hard. We pulled the drill up and let it drop and it went kerplunk but did nothing. We drilled and drilled for at least half an hour and the drill didn't go a bit further down in the hole. Then all of sudden, just as we were about to give up, it seemed to drop and get stuck. We had to pull and pull to get it back out again. We dropped it again and this time it went down about four or five feet. We tried it again and it did the same thing.

"We've hit a pocket of some kind. There's a hollow down there," I told Midge.

We pulled the bit out and tried to look down in the

hole with a flashlight. We couldn't see a thing. Now I realize that we should have looked at the bottom of the drill bit. However, we didn't know that then. The trouble with using that old buggy axle for a drill bit was that it makes a hole only about two inches in diameter and you can't see very well or very far in a small hole like that. A professional well-drilling rig like the one Mr. Marble is using drills a hole seven or eight inches in diameter and you can lower a bucket to find out if you've struck any water. But our hole was too small for that.

"We need a pipe or a hose of some kind and a pump," I said.

"We've got half a length of plastic hose that we can have, I'm sure," Midge said. "Dad cut it in two with a rotary lawnmower last month."

She went over to her house and got the hose and began poking it down the hole. It kept going down and down until I was certain that we hadn't drilled nearly that deep. We didn't have enough rope. We decided that there must be a regular cave or hole down there.

We didn't have any pump, so I decided to try sucking on the end of the hose. It was quite a job. I would suck on it for a while and then hold my hand over the end of the hose while I rested. Mr. Marble says that when you first get water from the well, it's always muddy. I expected to get a mouthful of muddy water but I wasn't prepared for what I got. All of a sudden I had a whole

111

mouthful of oil! It was awful-tasting stuff and I spit it out all over the grass. I was so surprised that I forgot to clamp my hand over the end of the hose and all the oil I had pulled up naturally went back down.

"It's oil!" I said when I could stop coughing and spitting.

"We've struck oil! We're millionaires!" Midge yelled. "Whoopee!"

I looked at the bottom of the bit, which was lying on the ground a few feet away, and it was covered with a film of oil, all right. Then Midge and I pulled the hose back up from the hole and looked at the bottom of it. Naturally as it came back up through the muddy hole the oil and mud had got mixed, but there was no mistaking it. There was oil down there. We found an old tin can and I ran my fingers over the bottom four or five feet of the hose and squeezed off a mixture of oil and mud into the tin can. There was enough of a sample there to prove definitely that we had made a strike.

The trouble is that nobody seems to be much interested or to believe us. I guess it's always that way when you make an important discovery. Uncle Al stuck his finger in the mud-and-oil mixture and rubbed two fingers together.

"It feels greasy all right," he said. "But I don't think I'd go out and buy any Cadillacs right away if I were you."

Midge's father, who is a research chemist, says it's not impossible that we could hit oil but he doubts seriously that we could hit it so near the surface. Midge kept insisting and so he has agreed to bring home a little hand pump from the laboratory. He has to go back this evening to finish some sort of experiment and he said he would bring the pump back with him, so we'll have it the first thing in the morning.

Thursday, July 11th

Midge and I were right. We did strike oil. There wasn't quite as much there as we had expected, but we hit oil all right. Uncle Al was right too about saying it was not advisable to try and buy up all the land around here.

It was ten o'clock before we were set to try pumping our well. News certainly gets around in a tiny place like Grover's Corner. I don't know how everybody heard about our oil well, but a crowd appeared out of nowhere. I guess people weren't quite as doubting as they acted. Aunt Mabel came over, Midge's mother, almost every other housewife in Grover's Corner, the man who was driving the bulldozer where the new house is being built, the milkman, the man who picks up laundry, and even Mr. Marble shut down his drilling rig for a little while. I don't know whether someone called the newspaper or whether Mr. Sylvester just happened by. He is the man who took the pictures of the buggy and the bathtub. Anyhow, he was on hand when we connected up the pump. We put the hose down in the well and set the little hand pump on a box, and I began pumping. Midge held a big galvanized steel bucket.

114

At first the connection wasn't tight and the pump kept sucking air. Then Mr. Marble tightened it and I tried pumping again. I had made about ten or twelve strokes when oil spouted out and into the bucket. Instead of everybody cheering as I'd expected, they all looked sort of silly. Mr. Marble said, "Well, I'll be a horned toad!" I pumped the bucket about half full and then stopped. Mr. Sylvester stepped forward, stuck his finger in the bucket, and held it up to his nose. Then he rubbed his fingers together as Uncle Al had done the night before. "It's oil," he said. "You kids really have discovered oil!"

Everybody began to get excited at this point. There was a lot of noise and two or three of the women rushed back home to telephone their friends. I guess everybody in that area would have been drilling wells in their back yards inside of another fifteen minutes if it hadn't been for Midge's father.

Mr. Glass had worked until two o'clock at the laboratory, so he didn't go to work this morning but slept late. I guess he got up about ten and found that he was alone in the house. He went downstairs and had some toast and coffee, and then, noticing the crowd across the street, came over to investigate. Instead of sticking his finger in the oil as everyone else had done, he picked up a stick and stirred it a little and let it drip back into the bucket.

"Oil!" Midge said, gloating. "I'll be known as the oil queen of New Jersey."

"It's oil, all right," Mr. Glass admitted. "It's been ten years since I had much to do with oil and I never was an expert, but just off-hand I'd say this wasn't crude oil. It looks more like one of the lighter grades of bunker fuel oil."

Mr. Ainsworth, who is an elderly retired plumber who lives two doors from Midge, started laughing. "That's what it is," he said. "It's fuel oil. There's a fuel-oil tank under here. I remember when it was put in. That was at

least twenty-five years ago. I think Jake Harris had the first oil burner in the township. That's a thousand-gallon tank down there. The house stood right over there. About where you're standing, Emma, would be the furnace room."

"It must be buried awfully deep," objected the milkman who watched me put the hose down the hole we had drilled.

"It wasn't this deep originally," Mr. Ainsworth explained. "This ground was fairly level then. This little hill where we're standing wasn't here at all. The ground right here was no higher than over there by the barn. Then when the highway department made that cut-off by the corner, they wanted some place to dump the dirt and Harris let them dump it here. They graded it off and put some topsoil over it. That's when the foundation of the house got buried."

Everybody just melted away. A few of them said something about being sorry, but as soon as they discovered we hadn't really brought in an oil well they weren't interested much any more. Mr. Marble slapped me on the back and said, "Cheer up, son. You struck a lot more oil than most wildcatters do when they first start."

After a minute there was only Midge, myself, Mr. Glass, and Mr. Sylvester left. Mr. Sylvester had been taking pictures, and he took one more with nobody standing by the pump except Midge and me.

118

"Well, whether it's bunker oil or crude oil, there is some oil down there," he said. "What are you going to do with it?"

"Let's measure and see how much is in there," Mr. Glass suggested.

We found a long stick and poked it down the hole. Mr. Glass looked at the mark on the stick and said, "If that's a thousand-gallon tank down there, there should be at least three hundred gallons in it. I don't know how many years it's been there, but it looks perfectly okay. I'll take a chance on it. If you can get it out I'll pay you the current price for fuel oil."

Mr. Glass and Mr. Sylvester walked off together, leaving Midge and me alone with our oil well. Then Midge turned and started toward her house.

"Where are you going?" I asked.

"Over to call the oil company," she said. "I want to find out how much fuel oil is."

She came back in a few minutes and told me that it was fifteen cents a gallon. That meant that if we had three hundred gallons we had forty-five dollars worth of oil. We weren't millionaires but forty-five dollars is a lot more than nothing, and at fifteen cents a gallon I'll be willing to pump the oil out with a hand pump and carry it across the street in buckets if necessary.

Tuesday, July 16th

Our research organization was on the front page of the *Princeton Bugle* again. There were pictures of all the people gathered around our oil well and an article about our striking oil and then finding out that we didn't have an oil well after all. The heading said "Great Oil Strike Proves Strikeout." I don't think much of either the headline or the article, and the next time I see Mr. Sylvester I'm going to tell him so. Research is a serious, dignified business, and it doesn't do you any good to have a newspaper article sort of poking fun at you. There was a long account about how Midge was a douser and could locate both oil and water. There was a picture of her holding a dousing rod. She was pleased as can be with both her picture and the article, and said that any publicity is always good publicity, but I don't agree. It's just as well that we haven't caught that white rabbit and that her name isn't part of the firm's name.

We got two hundred sixty-five gallons of oil out of the tank. There was a little bit more than that but the bottom was thick with sludge and Mr. Glass didn't think he'd better try using it. We pumped it up out of the tank by hand and into a fifty-five-gallon steel drum, which we carried in the cart behind Uncle Al's garden tractor. It took us three days to get all the oil out, but it was worth it. Today we got a check from Mr. Glass for thirty-nine dollars and seventy-five cents. We had another five dollars and thirty cents which we've made so far from the worms and pigeons, so we kept five dollars and five cents cash and put forty dollars in the bank in Princeton. Aunt Mabel went in to do some shopping right after lunch so Midge and I went along and opened the account. I wanted to put it in an account under the firm name but this caused a lot of complications, and finally Aunt Mabel, after talking it over with some man, suggested that we open two separate accounts under each of our names and divide up the money. The teller said, "Oh, you two are the kids who drilled the oil well, are you?" and looked at us as though we were something out of a zoo. I don't know why he should have, because if any town is full of odd-looking people and freaks it's Princeton, New Jersey. My father was at the consular office in Paris before we went to Naples and I thought I saw some odd-looking people there. They don't compare with Princeton. Professors wearing shorts pedal down the street on English bicycles with their beards waving out behind them, and nobody even bothers to turn around. Midge and I may have hit an old oil tank and thought we had an oil well, but at least we look fairly normal. As a matter of fact that bank teller doesn't look too bright.

121

Wednesday, July 24th

We sold all but one of our turtles today. We have had nine for some time and all they've done is sit around and eat and cause work. Agony seems better at locating turtles than he is at scaring up rabbits, but we've had so many that I haven't bothered to pick up the last two or three we've found. I couldn't think of any way they could be used for research purposes, or any other purpose for that matter. But if you really make up your mind to do something you can do it. This morning I made up my mind to get rid of the turtles.

"We either have to think up some way to use them, or some market for them, or I'm going to let them loose," I told Midge.

"*I* know," Midge said. "We could make turtle soup. We can use a different recipe with each turtle and maybe some soup company would pay us for the recipes."

"I don't think these are the kinds of turtles you make soup out of," I said. "They're probably edible, but you make soup from terrapins and snappers."

"Maybe we can sell them to some hair-tonic company," she suggested.

"What for?"

"Their backs look just like my father's bald head. If a hair tonic would grow hair on a turtle it ought to work on a man's head."

She was just being silly, of course, but now and then one of her silly ideas is a good one. "A turtle is useful," I said, thinking out loud. "They eat slugs and grubs. Maybe we could sell them to somebody to put in their flower garden."

"My mother is serving tea to the garden club this afternoon," Midge said. "If those turtles were a little bit prettier maybe we could sell them to the garden-club members. I know—paint each one to look like a flower."

"Be serious," I said.

"I am being serious," Midge insisted. "You're a good artist. You can paint a pretty flower on the back of each turtle. Then, when we tell them they eat grubs and slugs as well, it'll be a cinch."

We didn't have anything else to do so we got three or four colors of paint from Uncle Al's garage, and two or three more from Midge's father's workshop, and I started painting. I don't know too much about flowers, but Midge brought over a half a dozen flower magazines and I copied from them. I painted a couple of hydrangeas, a chrysanthemum, and a peony that looked so good that Midge claimed it smelled like one. Then I painted three roses, which were fair, and two camellias.

"Well, you did a good job of the creative work," Midge said. "My mother always says men are best at creative work but women are the most practical. So now I'll do the practical part." She turned over each turtle and wrote 60¢ on some and 65¢ or 70¢ on others and 75¢ on the peony.

"Why don't you make them all the same price?" I asked. "They're all about the same size."

"That shows how much you know about retailing," Midge said. "You've got to have things different prices. Some women will want to buy the highest-priced one to show off, and others the lowest-priced one in order to get a bargain. Let's put them in a basket and go over and see what my mother thinks of them."

The Glasses' back yard slopes away from the house and they have graded it into three terraces. One of them is a sort of walled-in sunken garden. There is a low stone wall on all four sides and you go down into it by several broad stone steps. Facing the steps is a small lily pool. Around three sides of the plot there is a narrow border garden of perennial flowers. The rest of the area is velvety-smooth lawn. Mrs. Glass is quite proud of this part of their grounds and works very hard keeping it nice. Midge is not quite so fond of that terrace as her mother, because it's her job to dig up all the dandelions and plantains that show up in the lawn.

It was a nice day and naturally Mrs. Glass was having

her garden-club meeting in the little walled garden. She had set up a number of chairs and small tables around the area and it looked very pretty. A few of the chairs looked sort of close to the lily pond to me, but I figured it was none of my business and said nothing.

Mrs. Glass and two women who were helping her were bustling around, decorating the tables and hurrying and fussing the way people always do before a meeting. We dumped the turtles out in the center of an uncluttered spot of the lawn and then Midge called her mother over to look at them.

"Can't you see I'm busy?" Mrs. Glass asked. "Besides I'm not interested in looking at turtles right now."

"But these are very unusual turtles," Midge insisted. "They have been painted by a famous artist from Europe."

"What are you talking about?" Mrs. Glass asked.

"Just what I said," Midge replied. "An artist from Naples, Italy, painted these turtles especially for garden-club ladies. They're all hand done. I want to come over and sell them when everybody gets here. Some of them are sixty cents, some of them are sixty-five, some seventy, and some seventy-five cents."

"You will do nothing of the sort," said Mrs. Glass. "The garden-club members are my guests today. I'm not going to have you ask them to buy anything." She looked at me. "Or anyone else, either."

126

"But they'll love these," Midge said.

Finally Mrs. Glass and the two women came over to look at the turtles. "They're most unusual," Mrs. Glass said, "and very pretty, but you cannot sell them at my garden-club meeting."

"That's quite a novel idea," said one of Mrs. Glass's friends. "I'll take one of them."

She bought one, and so did the other woman and so did Mrs. Glass. Probably they did it just to get rid of us. I don't know. Anyhow we put the three turtles in a pasteboard box and put them in one corner of the back porch. Then I picked up the others and put them in the basket, and we took them back to their pen at the research center. I had just dumped them in when Agony let out a yowl and started across the lot. The white rabbit was sitting at the edge of the woods. This time Agony was able to keep Jedidiah from heading toward Mr. Apple's property, and he chased him through the woods and out into the alfalfa field beyond. Midge and I followed, running as fast as we could. That white rabbit can really run. He stretched out like a jack rabbit and even though Agony went faster than I'd ever seen him, he couldn't catch that rabbit.

We followed them across the alfalfa field and then the rabbit doubled back toward the lot again. At the edge of the woods he found a hole and ducked down in it. When we got there Agony was digging furiously and I could tell

127

by his expression he was so mad he was about to bust. I have tried digging that rabbit out of holes twice and it is no use. Those holes seem to go on forever. I think probably woodchucks dig them first. This white rabbit has located a whole series of them. I'm beginning to believe that he lets Agony chase him for the fun of it, then when he gets tired of running he ducks down a hole.

Midge and I went up and watched the men building the new house for a while and then went back to the barn.

"I forgot to make a mark," she said, and she made a big scratch on the side of the barn where she is keeping track of the number of times we have chased that white rabbit. It is now thirty-two.

"Hey, the littlest camellia is gone," Midge said.

I looked, and sure enough, there were only five turtles in the pen. Since we had sold three, there should have been six. We examined the pen carefully but there was no hole where that turtle could have possibly slipped out.

"Do you suppose somebody could have been here and have stolen it?" I asked.

"Maybe we left it over at my house," Midge said. "Did you count them?"

I hadn't counted them. I had just picked them up and put them in the basket. We decided that it was probably in Mrs. Glass's garden someplace, so went over to look

128

for it. As we rounded the corner of the house we saw that the garden club was still there. A woman in a blue flowered dress and a big straw hat with grapes on top of it was talking about foundation planting. As we turned around to leave she finished her speech and everyone clapped. Then they all started talking at once, and some got up to congratulate the speaker.

"I'm going to slip down and see if I can find that turtle," Midge said. "I don't trust that garden club."

"They wouldn't steal a turtle."

"No, but they'd step on it. He's such a little tiny turtle, and some of those garden-club members are just plain big, and most of them have big feet."

I stayed where I was and she slipped down, jumped over the wall, and began looking for the turtle. Everybody was talking so no one paid any attention.

I didn't really see all that happened, but one woman, who was undoubtedly one of those that Midge meant when she said that some of the members were awfully big, got up from her chair and picked up a big black leather bag that had been lying on the ground beside her. It was as big as a small suitcase but it had one of those straps that you hang over the shoulder and was really a purse, I guess. Holding the bag by its strap, she moved over several feet to talk to a woman who was standing by the lily pond. She raised her bag, sort of cradling it in her left arm, and then bent her head and began poking in

129

the bag with her right hand. It must have been open already and all she had to do was shove the flap back. Suddenly she let out a horrible shriek. She dropped the purse, jumped backward about three steps, and fell into the lily pond.

Everyone was too surprised to do anything. Meanwhile this poor woman was floundering on her back in the lily pond. There was nothing for her to grab and the sides of the pond were sloped so she couldn't roll over very easily. Besides, she was too fat to do much of anything for herself. No one seemed to know what to do or how to get her out of there. The only thing I could think of was to call a tow truck and I doubt if they would have liked that suggestion. I stayed where I was and laughed until my sides ached.

Mrs. Glass was the hostess and so she had to do something. Finally she did the only thing possible. She waded right out into the middle of the lily pond and grabbed the woman's left arm. Another woman was able to stand on the edge of the pool and take the other arm. They hauled, lifted, and puffed, and finally they hoisted her up out of there.

That woman certainly was a sorry-looking mess. There was water dripping from her hair, and her soaking-wet dress stuck to her like the skin of a sausage. Somehow or other, her hat had managed to stay on her head through it all. It was a little straw hat with a lot of flowers on it. These sort of hung down over the edge of the hat like the strings of a mop. Water dripped off of them down onto her shoulders and back. Huffing and puffing, she walked forward about eight or ten steps, and then suddenly she fainted. Mrs. Glass and the other women tried to hold her up for a minute and finally gave up. They lowered her onto the grass and stood looking at her, huffing and puffing themselves. Mrs. Glass is a tiny little woman and I can see why she'd be tired. Someone said something about a doctor and one of the women started toward the house. Just then Midge joined me.

"I got the turtle," she announced.

"Did you ever see such a ruckus?" I asked. Even though the woman had fainted I couldn't help laughing.

Midge grinned. "It would be a lot funnier if she hadn't splashed half of my goldfish out of that lily pond. Now I know what causes tidal waves."

"What started it all?" I asked.

"Let's take this turtle over to the barn and I'll tell you," Midge answered.

"Let's wait and see if this woman comes to."

Midge shook her head. "Let's get away while the getting's good."

We walked across the street and put the turtle in the pen. "The reason I didn't want to stay any longer," Midge said, "was the turtle was what started it all. It was in her pocketbook."

131

The only thing we could figure out was that the turtle had been crawling around trying to escape all those women and had hunted for some place to hide. This woman must have laid her bag on the ground and it wasn't shut. The turtle probably thought it was a nice, dark place to hide and crawled in. Then later, when she picked up the purse and threw back the flap, there it was staring her in the face. If his head was out of his shell she might even have thought it was a snake. With the shell painted like a camellia she probably wouldn't have recognized it as a turtle. Besides, even if she had, it was probably startling to find a turtle in her purse.

A few minutes later we heard a siren screeching and then the first-aid car of the Hopewell Fire Department came roaring down the road. It turned in at Midge's house and two men got out. We waited a few minutes and then slipped across the street again. We kept out of sight behind the bushes and managed to get to the garage. We could see everything from there.

The first-aid squad wasn't needed after all. The woman was conscious and was up sitting in the chair, and the two men in the first-aid car were about to leave. Midge and I decided that we'd better do the same so we started across the street once more. The ambulance pulled out of the driveway just as we reached the edge of the road. A red and white sedan coming from the direction of Princeton pulled up abreast of us and a woman leaned over and rolled down the window. "I hope there's nothing wrong at your house, is there, Margaret?"

"Nothing serious, Mrs. Detweiler," Midge replied. "Mother's entertaining the garden club and one of the members fell into the lily pond."

"Goodness me!" said Mrs. Detweiler. "What was the subject of today's meeting, aquatic plants?"

"I don't know," Midge replied, "but I bet it's the most exciting meeting they've had in a long time."

Mrs. Detweiler looked at the sign on the end of the barn. "I've been reading about your research organization," she said. "It seems to be quite an enterprising business."

"Say, you're just the person who would like one of our turtles," Midge said. "Come over and look at them."

Mrs. Detweiler was quite taken with the turtles and she bought two for herself and three for friends. That left us only the peony, which Midge had decided we should keep for ourselves. It was a fairly good day's business.

My Aunt Mabel hadn't been at the garden-club meeting but naturally she heard all about it. When anything happens in a small place like Grover's Corner everyone knows about it sooner or later and usually it's sooner. Aunt Mabel told Uncle Al about it that night at dinner and he thought it was as funny as I had.

"It really isn't a laughing matter," Aunt Mabel said. "She might have been hurt."

"Was she?"

"No. Fortunately she wasn't. It was quite a shock to the poor woman, though. Her husband had to bring her some dry clothes and it was most embarrassing."

"You should have seen her threshing around in that lily pond," I said. "She splashed most of the water out onto the grass."

Uncle Al looked at me peculiarly. "Were you there?" he asked.

"Midge and I went over to hunt for something," I said. "We thought the meeting would be over."

"I see," he said. "How far were you from the woman when she fell into the pond?"

"I was way up by the corner of the house," I replied.

"She claims that she saw some sort of animal in her purse. She was startled, stepped back, and fell," Aunt Mabel explained.

Uncle Al nodded and looked at me again peculiarly, but he didn't say a word. In fact he changed the subject completely.

"You know, a curious thing happened here a couple of weeks ago," he said. "I was talking to one of the state troopers today. It seems that Mrs. Apple thought someone had stolen her cat. A dog chased it completely around her house and then she said a man poked a net through the hedge, caught the cat, and made off with it. When the trooper arrived there came the cat walking across the lawn."

134

"Was it stolen?" Aunt Mabel asked.

"Evidently not," Uncle Al replied. "Besides, it's been out here killing birds in our front yard since."

"What do you suppose it was all about?"

"I wouldn't know," Uncle Al replied. "It's just one of those things that happen. Maybe it's sunspots causing all this activity."

Sunday, July 28

Almost a month has gone by since I put my advertisement in the paper about Agony. I wonder how long people keep old newspapers around. I doubt if anyone is going to claim Agony now that so much time has gone by.

Monday, July 29th

I have half a notion to write the postmaster general and tell him what I think of the way the mail is being handled at Grover's Corner. I suppose most rural mail carriers are pretty nice people, but the one who delivers the mail to us isn't very cooperative or very intelligent for that matter. Of course, from the things he said, I guess he doesn't think much of Midge or me either, so things are about balanced.

For the past two or three days we haven't had even one rabbit. Midge had the idea that if we let Mathilda out of the pen to run loose, she might decoy Jedidiah back with her.

"And she might get as wild as he is," I objected.

"Not if we don't leave her out too long," Midge said. "I've let her go several times and she lets me walk right up to her."

I finally agreed, because one rabbit alone isn't much good when you want to raise rabbits to sell. Anyhow, we let Mathilda out. Midge was right; at first she was able to walk up to the rabbit without much trouble. For a while it looked as if the scheme might work. That evening, about

137

dusk, Mathilda came hopping up to the pen and Jedidiah was with her. We had left one end of the pen open and the plan was to wait until they were both inside eating, and then to slip up and close the opening. Jedidiah went inside and he seemed hungry. However, he wasn't so hungry that he forgot to keep an eye on us. Midge was within three feet of the pen when he bolted out and ran for the tree.

We left the pen open, and I suppose Mathilda hopped back out after she had eaten. We saw them several times yesterday but we didn't get very close. I don't know whether Mathilda had decided she liked freedom too or was just following Jedidiah, but she hopped away too. Midge began to get worried.

"He's a bad influence," she said. "I should never have let Mathilda go out with him."

This morning about ten-thirty, as I was walking toward the lot, I saw both rabbits beneath a rose bush in the Millers' front yard. I hurried to the barn to get a net and then over to get Midge for help. She got her father's fishing net and came along.

Both rabbits were facing the same way, and I don't know whether they were dozing or not, but we crept up quietly until we were only a few feet behind them. They didn't move. We have had a lot of practice trying to catch Jedidiah with a hand net, so I suppose we had to do it right sooner or later. We both pounced at once. Our timing was perfect and Midge got one rabbit and I got the other.

"Hurrah! I'm a member of the firm!" Midge shouted.

I had caught Mathilda and Midge had Jedidiah. I reached in and got Mathilda by the nape of the neck and pulled her out of the net, kicking and squirming like mad. A big rabbit like that is not easy to hold. Finally I got her cradled in my left arm, still holding onto the loose skin of her neck with my right hand. Then she quieted down.

Midge had a much rougher time. Jedidiah was wild, and he wasn't giving up without a fight. He kicked and ripped a hole in the net. Afraid that he would ruin the net, Midge lifted him out. He came out easily enough, but then he really began acting up. Her arms were bare and in a couple of seconds he had scratched her left arm so badly in several places that it was all over blood.

"I can't hold him much longer," she said. "What will I do?"

We were standing beside the Millers' mailbox. Grover's Corner is on a rural mail route, and everyone has sheet-metal mailboxes on posts out beside the road. The Millers' mailbox is a big one, and suddenly it occurred to me that we could use it.

"Stuff him in there," I suggested.

Midge yanked open the mailbox, shoved Jedidiah inside, and slammed the lid shut again. The lid fits tightly, so we weren't worried about the rabbit getting out. Carrying Mathilda, we headed back toward the barn.

We had to close the end of Mathilda's pen before we put her in it, and then we went over to Midge's to locate something to use in carrying Jedidiah back. We weren't satisfied with an ordinary pasteboard box because we didn't want to take any chances. Finally we found an old peach basket with a lid.

We were gone about five minutes. When we got in sight of the mailbox again, we saw a Willys Jeep station wagon belonging to the mailman parked in front of it.

"Don't open the mailbox!" we both shouted and we started running down the road.

We were too late. Mr. Mason, the mailman, opened the mailbox just as we yelled. He had driven up close to the box. He rolled down his car window and opened the lid. He was about to shove some letters in the box when the rabbit jumped out, practically in his face. Since the open car window was only about a foot away, naturally Jedidiah went right through it. He landed half on the steering wheel and then tumbled into Mr. Mason's lap.

The rabbit wasn't as surprised as Mr. Mason, and he recovered sooner. He scrambled out of Mason's lap and onto the seat beside him. Mr. Mason had a big pile of letters stretched out on the seat, all arranged according to his route. What that rabbit did to that mail shouldn't happen to anyone. It was scattered all over the seat and floor

140

as though a hurricane had hit it. Then Jedidiah jumped into the back, which was filled with packages and still more mail.

Mr. Mason let out a bellow and lunged over the seat after him. By this time I was standing at one front window looking in and Midge was at the other. There was a mad scramble in the back of the station wagon, with letters flying and packages sliding every which-way. Jedidiah raced around like a crazy rabbit while Mr. Mason flailed around after him. Finally Mason made a dive and came up holding the rabbit by his ears.

"You caught him," Midge shouted. "Good for you. I'll take him."

Mr. Mason climbed back over the front seat, puffing and red-faced. Still holding the rabbit by the ears, he shoved him through the open front window. I was hurrying around the front of the car to Midge's side because I had the basket. Before I got there, the rabbit doubled up his hind legs and kicked. Two long red scratches appeared on Mr. Mason's arm. He gave a bellow of pain and let the rabbit drop. Midge tried to catch him but she didn't get a good grip. The rabbit gave a mighty kick and shot out of her hands into the bushes.

"Why'd you drop him?" Midge demanded.

"Because the vicious little beast was ripping me to pieces," Mason said angrily, looking at his arm.

"Now we'll never get him," Midge said disappointedly.

142

"You might at least have held him a second longer."

"If you think you've got troubles, look at this car," Mason said. "I spent two hours sorting that mail, and now look at it. Well, you two can tell anybody that asks, that this route is going to be mighty late in getting its mail today." He glared at the scattered mail. "Two hours' work wasted!"

"We've had weeks of work wasted," I said. "That's how long we've been chasing that rabbit."

"Well, you certainly picked a fine place to put him when you did catch him," Mason said.

"We just put him there until we could get back with this basket," I said.

"He was a male rabbit," Midge said very innocently.

For a minute I thought Mr. Mason was going to explode. Then he put his hands on the edge of the window and leaned part way through. He stuck his jaw out and said, "If I find that male rabbit in another mailbox, I'll stamp him, and good!"

Tuesday, July 30th

Not too much has happened since my last entry. I went with the Glasses to the outdoor movies last night, which I enjoyed a lot. It was the first time I had ever been to one. I've never seen an outdoor movie in Europe although I understand that one is being built near Rome. I was talking to the man who runs the place and he said he thought outdoor movies had some pretty serious problems in Europe. I asked him why and he said because of the midget cars. He's having trouble here in the United States with customers who come in Volkswagons and other little cars. They can't see over the Cadillacs. He thinks he's either going to have to put in a special children's section for the small cars, or provide them with jacks so they can raise themselves up in the air. I told him I didn't think the last solution would be very sensible because people would have trouble getting in and out of the car doors and his popcorn sales would fall way off. Then he and Midge started laughing. I don't know what about because it sounds like a real problem.

The reason we went to the outdoor movies was that we didn't have any lights in Grover's Corner last night. The reason we didn't have any lights is connected in a way with our research organization.

The Ainsworths, who live down near where the new house is being built, had a wasps' nest in a mulberry tree out near their chicken house. Midge heard about it and went over to look at it several days ago. It was one of those great big gray paper nests that wasps build and I'd only seen one of them before. Most of the wasps around here just build sort of open cones underneath the eaves of buildings and don't make a paper covering around them. This was one of the biggest wasps' nests I've ever seen, even bigger than the ones in the Museum of Natural History when I visited there two years ago.

"I'd like to have that," I said.

"Why?" Midge asked. "Is it full of honey?"

I explained that wasps don't store honey like bees do. They kill spiders and flies and store them away instead. Midge doesn't know even the simplest facts about insects and animals.

"Then what do you want it for?" Midge asked.

"I'd like to look at it," I said. "The wasps knew how to make paper before people did. Besides we might be able to sell it."

"Who would want a wasps' nest?" Midge asked.

"A museum," I replied.

She didn't think much of the idea, but I asked Mrs. Ainsworth if she minded if I took the wasps' nest. She said certainly not. In fact she would gladly pay me a dollar if I would take it away. Midge was a little more in favor of the idea then and agreed to help me.

"We could hang it up near the barn," I said, "and the wasps would eat all the spiders on the second floor."

"Nothing doing," Midge said flatly. "There's not room enough in this firm for the wasps and me, too. Have you ever been stung by a wasp?"

I'd never been stung by a wasp, although I have been stung by bees. Midge said it wasn't the same thing at all. Finally I agreed that we wouldn't try to preserve the wasps, just the nest. We found a five-gallon pretzel tin that seemed like the perfect container, and we went over to get the nest.

I borrowed Mrs. Ainsworth's ladder and got it up against the tree without any trouble. I was about two-thirds of the way up the ladder with a saw in my hand, planning to saw off the limb where the nest hung, when I got stung. Midge was right. A wasp's sting is nothing like a bee's sting. It really hurts. I decided right then and there that I wasn't going to get the nest until I had the proper equipment.

I asked Uncle Al that night if he knew where I could buy a can of the smoke that beekeepers use. Naturally he wanted to know what I was going to use it for. I told him that I wanted to get rid of some wasps.

146

"Your mother liked bees and you like wasps," he said, shaking his head. "I suppose you'll be stung less if you have the smoke than if you don't have it. Frankly, my advice is to stay as far away from wasps as possible. I have put off painting the eaves of that garage out there for two years because of those wasps."

He got me the smoke yesterday morning and I got out my mother's old bee equipment. The net was full of holes, but Aunt Mabel made me a new net out of an old curtain. The net is attached to the hat at the top and comes down over my shoulders. There are two drawstrings to pull it tight around your chest and under the arms. After I got the net on, I put on a jacket and some long gloves and then I was practically sting-proof.

I tried out my suit first on the wasps' nests under the eaves of Uncle Al's garage. These weren't the kind of wasps that build the big paper nests, of course, and they weren't very interesting, but my net worked perfectly and I didn't bother using any smoke. I simply climbed up on the stepladder and knocked all the cones down. The wasps buzzed around my head, as mad as could be, but they couldn't get through to sting me.

Next we went over to Mrs. Ainsworth's and I put up the ladder again. I climbed up to the top, not paying any attention to the wasps. When I got up to the nest I gave it several shots from my smoke can. I wasn't worried about them stinging me but I knew that when I started sawing off the limb they would really get mad. Midge was holding the ladder and she didn't have any net.

Everything went perfectly, which shows that if you plan in advance you can do almost anything without any trouble. I sawed off the outer end of the limb first, then sawed it again between the tree and the nest. That left the nest hanging to the little piece of limb, about a foot long, which I was holding.

I had poked a tiny hole in the top of the pretzel-can lid and had threaded a little piece of wire through this. I climbed down with the nest, hung it to the little wire loop in the lid, and put the lid carefully on the can. Midge had retreated to the corner of the house where she stood watching.

There were quite a few wasps who were out hunting, and I stood there for a few minutes watching them as they came back. They looked pretty silly zooming in, expecting to find a great big nest and instead finding nothing but empty space. I suppose a person would feel the same way if he arrived home to find that a hurricane had blown away his house. I felt a little bit mean, because I certainly played those wasps a dirty trick.

I felt even sorrier for the wasps that were in the nest inside the can. They were prisoners and would starve to death. At least the others could start over again. Midge didn't seem to feel a bit sorry for any of them, though.

She said that she hoped all of them got their stingers doubled over trying to sting the tin can.

I picked up the can and we started back toward the barn. As we passed the new house we noticed that the bulldozer was digging another hole off to one side of the house.

"Maybe they're going to have a swimming pool," Midge said hopefully. "But I don't know why they didn't start on that first instead of the house. Half the summer's gone."

"I doubt if it's a swimming pool," I said. "It doesn't look big enough."

"Then what is it?"

The bulldozer was digging dirt out of the hole and pushing it into a low spot up near the front of the lot. "Wait until he comes back up here and we'll ask him," I said.

I set the can down beside the road and climbed up the bank to watch the bulldozer. Midge joined me a minute later. The bulldozer came chugging toward us, and Midge waved her hand.

"Is that a swimming pool?" she shouted.

"No such luck," the driver shouted back. "Digging out for the footing for a garage."

He had stopped the bulldozer to answer Midge but now he started again, distributing the dirt around evenly along the front part of the lot. A plumber's truck came tearing down the road and turned in the driveway. The man was driving much faster than he should have been, and I suppose he didn't realize that he had reached the driveway until the last minute. He slammed on his brakes, his tires screeched, and he skidded around the turn into the driveway. I had set the pretzel can well out of the way, I thought; it would have been for any ordinary driver, but not for this cowboy. His rear bumper just touched the pretzel can, but that was enough to knock it over. It rolled down into the ditch and the lid came off.

"Look out! Wasps!" Midge shouted at the top of her voice, and she took off like a streak for the back of the lot.

I had put my bee hat and net and gloves and can of smoke on top of the pretzel can when I'd set it down beside the road. They fell down in the ditch with the can and I couldn't get to them. I waited a few seconds but when I saw those wasps coming out of that can like a black cloud I decided to follow Midge.

"Look out! Those are wasps!" I yelled to the bulldozer driver in case he hadn't heard Midge.

He said later that he hadn't heard either one of us. The first thing he knew about the wasps was that he had been stung on the neck. They zoomed in on him like a bombing squadron and were all around him at once. He started swinging his arms around like mad and then he noticed that he was headed for the ditch. He gave the wheel a yank and started swinging at the wasps again. By this time they were really after him. Later he counted fifteen wasp stings, so I suppose most of the time he didn't know what was happening. Finally he decided that the only thing to do was to stop the bulldozer and to get out of there. By that time it was too late. Just as he stopped it, it banged against the light pole beside the driveway. The bulldozer wasn't going fast but the ground was soft beside the light pole, and it was just a temporary pole. It didn't break off but it leaned over at about a forty-five-degree angle. It reached far enough to hit against the main lines at the road and snap one of them.

By this time the wasps had reached the house, and they were still after blood. They chased the mason and the two carpenters out of there and stung all three of them. The man who had caused all the trouble, the plumber, didn't get stung at all.

After a few minutes passed, I found a long stick and I slipped back out by the road. I managed to get my hat and net and put these on. Then I walked down into the ditch, got my gloves, and put the lid back on the can. Most of the wasps had left the nest. It had broken into three or four pieces. I was pretty sore at that plumber for ruining my wasps' nest but there wasn't much point in complaining. I couldn't ask him to pay for the nest because I didn't know what it was worth. I decided to say nothing. Besides, I thought it might be just as well if that bulldozer operator didn't know where the wasps came from.

I dumped what remained of the nest out in the alfalfa

field in back of the lot and put away my bee equipment. I hadn't seen a sign of Midge since the can was knocked in the ditch. As I came out of the barn she came across the street.

"Where have you been?" I asked.

"I went back to collect that dollar from Mrs. Ainsworth," she said. "I thought maybe I'd better get it before she tried to cook dinner tonight."

"What's that got to do with it?"

"She's got an electric stove," Midge said. "In case you haven't heard, there isn't any power in Grover's Corner."

She was right. Somebody phoned the power company and they promised to be out as soon as they could but they hadn't appeared yet at dusk and everybody in Grover's Corner last night ate dinner by candlelight. Of course some people couldn't even cook dinner at home because they had electric stoves, so they went out to restaurants. Aunt Mabel has a bottle-gas stove so it didn't make much difference at our house. The Glasses have an electric stove but Mr. Glass grilled a steak outside on the charcoal grill.

Mr. Glass had planned to do some work on a scientific paper that he is writing, but since there weren't any lights he decided to take the family to the outdoor movies and they invited me to go along. The power company worked fast, and by the time we got back from the movies there were lights again.

152

Thursday, August 1st

We had more trouble with Mr. and Mrs. Apple today. I'm beginning to agree with Midge that there's something very mysterious about him. Maybe he does have a body buried over there or maybe he's a counterfeiter or something; but he certainly doesn't like people around. He seems to have a phobia about anybody or anything coming near his place. The other day when the man from the power company came in to read the meter I asked him if he ever saw anything mysterious over at the Apples'. He said the meter was outside, and since he hadn't ever been in the house he didn't know whether there was anything mysterious there or not.

Siegfried was what caused the trouble. I don't dislike the cat the way Midge does, but he is a nuisance. He's always over on our lot stalking birds or trying to get up in the barn to catch pigeons. We chase him away but I'm not mean to him because I know cats just naturally like to eat birds, just as birds naturally like to eat worms.

The white rabbit's score is now forty-one. Midge says when she reaches fifty she's going to give up. I'm not. I'm stubborn, and I think Agony feels the same way. Every time he sees that white rabbit he takes off like a shot. Several times he's even taken off after pieces of white paper. I think he figures that it's a private war between himself and that rabbit.

The big circle of wire that we set up as a sort of trap wasn't any good. The rabbit dug a tunnel under it when we weren't watching and the one time that we did manage to catch him inside the wire he let us chase him around a few times and then ducked out through the hole.

One of the books in the nature library in my room has a section in it about traps. I read this through and then made a box trap. A box trap is simply a wooden box with a sliding door. The door is held up in the air and attached to a trigger at the back of the box. When the animal goes inside the box it touches the trigger and the door drops down behind him. There is nothing about the trap that can hurt an animal. He may get a little thirsty by the time you come to let him out, but since the trap is usually baited with a piece of corn or something like that, an animal like a rabbit would even have something to eat while he waited.

I finished the trap yesterday and set it near the rabbit pen, thinking that maybe Jedidiah might come over now and then to visit Mathilda. There was nothing in the trap yesterday morning or this morning either, and Midge claimed that it was no good. However, I didn't expect to find anything. It takes several days or even longer for the

154

human smell to disappear from a trap and still longer for most animals to find the courage to go into something new and strange.

Of course, there is no way of knowing when you set a box trap what you're going to catch. Uncle Al was right about that lot. You are apt to see most anything there. So far I've seen wild rabbits, woodchucks, skunks, squirrels, and raccoons. Of course, there are all different kinds of birds—cardinals, blue jays, thrushes, robins, chickadees, grackles, and sparrows. The best time to see birds is very early in the morning. That's a good time to see animals, too. Several times I have set my alarm for five-thirty and gone for a walk in the woods, but most of the time I take a walk right after breakfast. Uncle Al gets up fairly early and we are usually finished with breakfast by seven-fifteen or seven-thirty. I leave Agony tied up at home because he scares everything. The Glasses are usually just eating breakfast at that time, so Midge isn't around, which is a good thing, too. She's always in too much of a hurry. You have to be very slow and quiet and patient to see wild animals.

Day before yesterday I finished breakfast a few minutes after seven and went over to the lot for my walk. I looked at the box trap but there was nothing in it, so I went on back into the woods. I saw two rabbits and a pheasant but not much else. Then as I was heading back toward the road over near Mr. Apple's property I

155

happened to look through the hedge. There in the middle of that big back lawn of his were three deer—a doe and two fawns. They were standing right in the middle of Mr. Apple's roped-off area, nibbling away at the grass as peaceful as could be.

I squatted down on my haunches and watched them for three or four minutes. Deer are beautiful animals. Even when they're not running they look speedy and graceful. Those three on that big smooth lawn looked like three statues. Now and then the doe would raise her head and gaze around with big, soft eyes. The two fawns would eat for a minute and then give several little playful jumps, almost like baby lambs.

I decided I would go across the street and find out if Midge was up because I knew she would want to see them too. I slipped away very quietly, crossed the street, and knocked on the Glasses' back door. Midge was just sitting down to breakfast but she decided that that could wait, she would rather see the deer. She ran into the next room and came back a minute later with a camera.

"If they're still there I'm going to take a picture," she said.

The deer were still there, although I don't know why. Midge stepped on three or four sticks and giggled twice. Uncle Al says that deer know when it is hunting season and are much less scary other times of the year. At any rate, the three deer were grazing at about the same spot when we returned. Midge focused her camera, got it all set, and then poked it through a small opening in the hedge and clicked the shutter. The doe heard the click and lifted her head suspiciously. She looked around for several minutes and then, seeing nothing, began eating grass again.

"I wish I had beautiful eyes like that," Midge whispered as she turned the film.

"Why?" I asked.

"I'd go to Hollywood."

"But if you had eyes like that deer you'd probably have ears and a nose like it, too," I said.

"I could still get a job at Walt Disney's studios," she said, and started to giggle.

The deer heard the giggle and looked over in our direction. That's probably why she didn't hear Mr. Apple, who came through the gap in the hedge in the front part of his lot. He was carrying a shotgun.

"Look," I said, jabbing Midge with my elbow.

Mr. Apple raised the shotgun and as he did so Midge poked her camera through the hole in the hedge again. She snapped the picture just a second before he fired. Then we heard the blast of the shotgun and the three deer jumped as though they had been hit. They hadn't, however, and all three of them took off across the lawn like three streaks, their white tails bobbing up and down as they went bounding toward the rear hedge. I guess they

157

had been on Mr. Apple's lawn several times before, because they seemed to know exactly where to find a hole to get through.

"Why, that stinker!" Midge said. "Shooting at those deer! Why, I'd be proud to have them on my lawn."

"I don't think he was trying to hit them," I said. "He was pointing pretty far up in the air."

"Well, why didn't he just yell at them then?" Midge asked. "There was no need to scare them out of a year's growth."

"I suppose that's his idea," I said. "To really scare them so they'll stay away."

Midge fumed and fussed about Mr. Apple. I didn't like the idea of his shooting at the deer either, because I like to have them around so I can watch them. However, my Uncle Al says that there are so many deer in New Jersey that they're getting to be pests. They eat up farmers' crops and the vegetable gardens of people who live in the country. He's even had trouble with them in his garden. There's a hunting season each fall but only for bucks. Uncle Al says the State Game Commission knows that the only thing to do is to have an open season on does but every time one is suggested the women's clubs in the state react just as Midge did. They start talking about the beautiful, helpless deer, and the Game Commission gets scared. Uncle Al says that while female deer may be helpless, the female of the human species certainly is not.

Midge went back home to have breakfast and I went home to do some chores for Aunt Mabel. About eleven o'clock Aunt Mabel drove over to New Hope to see a friend, and I went along. We didn't get back until after five. While Aunt Mabel was getting dinner Uncle Al and I walked down to the lot. Midge had said something about going to Trenton and I didn't know whether she had fed the rabbit or not.

As we approached the lot I heard voices, but I didn't think anything about it because there are people living on both sides and across the street. Then as we rounded the corner of the barn I heard a couple of bangs and I saw Mr. and Mrs. Apple. He was stomping on what remained of my box trap, which wasn't much.

"Hey, that's my trap!" I said.

Mr. Apple looked startled, but he didn't back down an inch. "I have just destroyed it," he said, shaking his head and drawing himself up as tall as he could, which isn't very tall.

Uncle Al looked at him as though he didn't believe what he'd heard. "And why, might I ask?"

"Because my poor cat has been a prisoner in it all day," said Mrs. Apple indignantly. "I've a good notion to report this to the SPCA. I don't know what this boy has against my cat, but it's quite obvious that he enjoys being mean to it."

"I didn't set that trap for your cat," I said. "I set it for Jedidiah, our white rabbit. It had a carrot in it. I don't know what your cat was doing, going in to get a carrot."

160

Uncle Al was beginning a slow burn. He drew a deep breath and said, "I might point out that the trap was not set on your property and that in order to be caught in it your cat had to be trespassing. I might also point out that you too are trespassing. This lad went to a lot of trouble to build that box trap, and your destroying it was entirely uncalled for. You claim that my nephew seems to have it in for your cat. I think it's the other way around. You seem to have it in for him."

"I have nothing against your nephew," said Mr. Apple, "or against this little girl here."

I turned around and there stood Midge. When she had appeared I don't know, but naturally she wasn't going to miss a good fight.

"These two children have created a public nuisance here on this lot," Mr. Apple continued. "From the minute that sign was painted on the end of the barn we have not had a moment's privacy. Half the day that dog is letting out unearthly sounds, and he seems to spend half his time chasing a white rabbit back and forth across my place, with these two children yelling encouragement. There is always some sort of chaos going on. The road has been blocked by strange contraptions and crowds have gathered because of some silly report about oil. People have parked in my driveway, tramped across my lawn, honked their horns in front of our door, and generally made our life miserable. The other night we had to do without power for several hours and I understand that this young man was indirectly responsible. We moved to the country for some privacy, Mr. Harris, and until your nephew appeared we enjoyed it."

"I like peace and quiet myself," Uncle Al said slowly. "I appreciate your desire for privacy. However, I don't think my nephew has trespassed on your property, have you, Hank?"

"I haven't set foot on the place," I said, "and neither has Midge."

"It is quite possible that the dog has run across your property several times, just as your cat has killed our birds," Uncle Al said. "As for other people tramping across your lawn or parking in your driveway, I'm sorry, but that is not my nephew's fault or responsibility. He didn't invite them here. While you have a right to your privacy, he has a right to the normal pursuits of a boy his age. If he wants to yell and chase a white rabbit, then as far as I'm concerned he can. He's on his own property here and he can yell his head off for all of me. In the future, stay off this property and don't do anything like smashing that box trap again or I'll take you to court."

"I would be very happy to be taken to court on the subject of the box trap," Mr. Apple said. "In case you haven't read the game laws, you might be interested to know that trapping rabbits is illegal in this state. I intend to make a report to the game warden that your nephew has been attempting to do that."

"I wasn't trying to trap wild rabbits. I was trying to trap a white rabbit that belongs to Midge."

"Trapping is trapping," said Mr. Apple.

"You go right ahead and tell the game warden," Uncle Al said. "I think he'll accept the boy's explanation."

"If the game warden comes to see me I'm going to tell him about your shooting at those deer this morning," I said.

Midge started laughing. "And I took a picture that will prove it."

"What's that?" Uncle Al asked.

"There were three deer out on his back lawn," I said. "He came out with a shotgun and shot at them."

"I was simply scaring them off the place," said Mr. Apple.

"The game warden might doubt that," Uncle Al said grinning. "In case you're interested, the usual fine for shooting deer out of season is at least a hundred dollars. Now, I'm not an informer, and I don't want to get my neighbors in trouble, but if you want to be mean, I can be just as mean. I suggest that we call this a draw. You go on home and mind your business and we'll mind ours."

Uncle Al sputtered and fumed all the way home. "I don't enjoy a fight like that," he said. "I'd much rather have pleasant relations with my neighbors, but

163

there's something wrong with that man. His conduct isn't normal."

"Midge says he's got bodies buried in his back yard."

Uncle Al chuckled. "Maybe he really has struck oil, and he's trying to keep it a secret."

Monday, August 5th

It rained most of the week end and I spent a good part of Saturday and Sunday in the house, reading. Late Sunday afternoon it began to clear and Uncle Al and I went outside. The rain had been quite heavy and the water had flooded down the driveway, washing half the gravel into the grass. He was completely disgusted.

"This has happened every time there's been a heavy rainstorm for the past ten years," he said. "Now there's a research project for you, or an engineering job, whatever you want to call it. Figure out some way that my driveway and maybe half the lawn doesn't get flooded every time there's a hard rain."

Although it had stopped raining, water was still flowing down the driveway. It came from a ditch beside the highway at the front of the place. When we walked up the road we saw that there was at least two feet of water in the ditch.

"The main trouble is that culvert there," said Uncle Al. "The water from our half of the road flows down on this side and into the ditch. It's supposed to go through that culvert and on down the other side of the road to the creek, but nine-tenths of the time the culvert is clogged. As a result we have a flood."

The culvert that he was talking about is really just a big corrugated galvanized steel pipe which runs underneath the road. "The trouble is it isn't big enough," I said.

"That is a very astute observation," said Uncle Al, "and it's one that I made about nine or ten years ago. I've made it at regular intervals to the highway department ever since. When I complain, they send a man out and he pokes a stick in there or something to get out the leaves and debris, and that's all. It works reasonably well for several rains and then clogs up again and we have the same trouble. The last three houses on this side of the road have had their front lawns flooded at least three or four times a year for I don't know how long."

"Couldn't you put some sort of a screen over this end?" I asked.

"I tried that," Uncle Al said. "Then the stuff just clogs up and blocks the entrance to the culvert. It's a little bit easier to clean away the debris that way, but that's all. It clogs up quicker and to keep the culvert operating I'd have to stand out here in pair of hip boots all the time it was raining. I don't want to do that. I prefer a roof over my head when it rains."

I said that I would give the problem my attention and I did. I thought about it several times but I couldn't figure out an answer, except, of course, to put in a much larger culvert. I did get a long bamboo pole from the garage and poked it through the culvert. I managed to dislodge a big glob of sticks and leaves and then the water began to go through much faster. However, there wasn't any doubt that Uncle Al was right and it would soon clog up again the next time it rained.

It was a nice day today, and while the ground was soft and wet I dug some earthworms and put them in the bathtub. Then, since we were out of straw, I got Uncle Al's tractor and cart and we went to Mr. Baines's farm for another bale. On the way back we stopped by the new house to watch them put up the roof rafters.

The man with the bulldozer had finished his work and was gone and only one of the carpenters who had been stung was still there. He wasn't sore at us any longer. I don't know why he was ever sore in the first place. After all, we couldn't know that that plumber was going to be such a reckless driver.

I had expected that we would have to keep Agony on a leash after our last talk with Mr. Apple, but Uncle Al said no. He warned me to keep the dog away from Mr. Apple's property as much as I could and said that we would wait and see what they did about their cat.

Agony disappeared someplace and I didn't pay too much attention. Then I heard his rabbit voice and I could tell from the tones that he was after the white rabbit again. That wouldn't have bothered me except that he was on the wrong side of the road.

The white rabbit goes back and forth across the road from Midge's house to my lot quite often. I don't know how he manages to avoid being run over by cars, and sometimes when I am annoyed I hope that he will be. I guess he is just as smart about avoiding cars as he is about not being caught. I don't worry about him but I do about Agony. Agony does not chase cars. He stays out of the road and when he crosses the road he's very careful about it. But when he starts chasing that rabbit he forgets there are such things as roads or cars. Several times he has located the rabbit on Midge's side of the street, and after chasing around over there for a while the rabbit invariably heads for my lot. I guess all the woodchuck holes, and the woods at the back, make that his safest place. Two or three times they have streaked across the road, neither one paying any attention to whether there are cars coming or not. Although there isn't much traffic on the road, one car is all that's needed. There would be a dead dog or dead rabbit.

As soon as I heard Agony barking on Midge's side of the road I started running down the road to locate him. I was about opposite Uncle Al's house when I heard him in the back yard of the Ainsworths'. At least that's where I thought he was. I was running in that direction when suddenly they came directly toward me. About fifteen seconds later, they went flashing by, headed for the road. I shouted for Agony but he didn't pay the slightest bit of attention.

I rushed through the shrubbery in front of the Ainsworths' just in time to see the rabbit tear down the bank with Agony close behind him. Agony was really giving Jedidiah a run for his money. He was only about three feet behind him and he was gaining. The rabbit was either tired or is getting fat. Of course he should be getting fat. He eats the best out of everybody's garden.

Instead of crossing the road the rabbit went straight along the bottom of the ditch. When he got opposite Uncle Al's he made a sudden and abrupt turn and disappeared in the steel culvert. Agony tried to stop but he skidded about three feet before he could turn around. Then he poked his nose in the culvert, hesitated for a minute, and disappeared inside.

I looked up and down the road. No cars were coming so I made a mad dash across to the other end of the culvert. I got there just too late. I was hoping that the culvert would be blocked and that the rabbit would be trapped inside, but he wasn't. I was almost there when he came scrambling out the end in front of Uncle Al's house. He was muddy and dirty and he was scared, but he got through. I made a leap for him and missed him. He hopped up the bank and disappeared in the rhododendrons in Aunt Mabel's front yard.

169

Midge had started the tractor and she drove up beside
me. "What happened?" she asked.

"Agony almost had the rabbit," I said. "He was gaining
on him fast when the rabbit ducked into this culvert."

"Agony is always gaining on him," Midge said. "The
trouble is he starts too far behind. Is the rabbit still in
the culvert?"

"No, he managed to get through," I said. "Agony hasn't
come out yet."

I leaned down to look in the culvert but it was black
inside. "Here, Agony," I called and Agony gave a whine.
I could hear him scratching but nothing else. "Come on,
boy," I called. "Come on out of there."

170

"I'd hide too if I couldn't catch a big fat pet rabbit,"
Midge said.

"He's not hiding," I said. "I think he's stuck."

I went to the other end of the culvert and called but
Agony didn't come out. Now and then I'd hear him scratching and he'd whine but we couldn't see a thing from either
end. I went inside the house and got a flashlight. I could
just see Agony's tail and hind end from one end of the
culvert and from the other I thought I could see the tip of
his nose, but I wasn't sure. I had poked out most of the
sticks Sunday afternoon but there was still plenty of dirt
inside, and leaves and other junk. I got a long pole and put
a wire on the end and managed to pull out an old rusty

tin can, but that didn't accomplish anything except to let me see a little better. Agony seemed to be stuck right in the middle of the culvert and I couldn't reach him with the pole from either end. Even if I had been able to reach him I couldn't have done anything except poke him.

"How in the world are we going to get him out of there?" Midge asked, getting worried.

"I don't know," I said. "I'll have to figure out some way."

I sat down by the edge of the road to think about the problem. Midge is the kind of girl who believes in action. She doesn't think you can accomplish anything while you're sitting still. Maybe her brain is connected to her arms and legs and won't move unless they do. She called Agony from first one end of the culvert, then the other. Then she poked around with the stick and practically burned out the flashlight. Since she had to get down on her knees in the ditch to look in the culvert and the bottom of the ditch was still muddy, she was certainly a sad-looking sight. She had mud all over her legs, her hands, her arms, and even her face. Finally she stuck her head inside the culvert to get a better look and came out really streaked with mud. To make matters worse she got something in her eye.

"Don't just sit there, you big boob," she said, half crying because of the dirt in her eye.

172

At that moment a woman in a green station wagon came driving by. Maybe she thought Midge had had an accident or something. Anyhow, she stopped.

"Is there anything wrong?" she asked.

"Agony's inside the culvert," Midge said, wiping the tears away from her eyes. "He's stuck and I can't get him out."

"Who's Agony?"

"A dog," Midge replied. "He went in after a rabbit and now he can't get out. I'm afraid he'll suffocate. Or if he doesn't do that, he'll starve in time."

"Are you certain that he can't get out?"

"He's right in the middle," Midge replied, "and we've called him and all he does is whine. I can't even touch him with this long pole."

The woman got out of her car to investigate or help— I don't know which. She had on a light tan silk dress and she was dressed to go somewhere special. She took one look at the mud in the ditch at both ends of the culvert and decided that she would take Midge's word for it. Just then Agony let out a howl that reverberated back and forth in the culvert, making an awful racket. Anyone who doesn't know beagles would have sworn that he was dying of pain.

"I wonder who would help," the woman said. "You call the fire department to get animals down from high places, and the police are usually helpful." She paused a moment, then said suddenly, "There were some men working about half a mile back on the highway."

She jumped in her car, turned around, and disappeared down the road. I took another look in the culvert but I couldn't see much. The flashlight gave only a weak glimmer. I went into the house to get two new batteries and by the time I came back the woman was back again.

"Don't you worry," she told Midge. "Those men will be here in a minute. They're finished whatever they're doing and were coming this way anyhow." Midge thanked the woman, who said she had an engagement to keep and drove on.

You often see repair crews of three or four men in a truck fixing holes in black-top roads. I thought that the woman had talked to a crew like that, but about five minutes later a whole procession came rumbling down the road.

"Holy Ned! We have an entire construction gang coming," I said to Midge.

In the lead was a station wagon, followed by three big trucks, one of those big air-compressor rigs, and a crawler power shovel loaded on a flatbed trailer. Way off in the distance was a huge roller chugging along slowly but steadily.

"Just pretend he's your dog," I told Midge. "Men always are more sympathetic with little girls than with boys. Act as though you're worried sick."

174

"I *am* worried sick," said Midge. "Aren't you?"

"Not particularly," I said. "Not now."

The station wagon pulled into Uncle Al's driveway and a man in a khaki shirt got out. "Where's this dog that's caught in a culvert?" he asked.

"Right in there," said Midge, doing a perfect job of looking anxious and forlorn. The man got down on his knees and looked in the end of the culvert where Midge was standing. She handed him the flashlight. "I can see his tail," he announced. He got up and came over to my end of the culvert and looked in there. "He has certainly got himself stuck in the middle, hasn't he? And *by* the middle too, it seems."

The three trucks had stopped by this time and the truck drivers were all gathered around. They seemed to think this was a big joke, and even Midge grinned a little. She has a peculiar sense of humor. The big air compressor and the truck hauling the power shovel pulled up beside the road and stopped. Mr. Ainsworth came out of his house and walked over to see what was going on. I could see that we were soon going to have a crowd.

The foreman, or whoever the man was who was in charge, got up from the ditch and brushed the dirt off his knees. "I don't know how to get him out of there except with a can opener," he said.

"That culvert looks pretty rusty," said one of the truck drivers.

175

"Yes, it's pretty well shot," the foreman agreed. "It's probably good for a couple of years more at the most." He looked at a short, stocky man wearing horn-rimmed glasses who had been driving the air compressor rig. "How long do you think it will take, Jim?" he asked.

The man rubbed his chin. "We could rip up the surface in half an hour or so and have that culvert out of there by four-thirty. The new culvert is apt to be the hitch. If that arrives the first thing in the morning we should have everything cleaned up and be away from here by eleven."

"Well, that won't be too bad. We're a little bit ahead of schedule anyhow, and I guess this classifies as a real emergency," the foreman said. "Take these two trucks on in but the rest of you start ripping this culvert out."

In less than ten minutes there were three men with air hammers cutting a strip from the black-top straight across the road. Another truck arrived, loaded with signs, and the foreman sent it off to put up detour signs at the two nearest corners. The power shovel was unloaded from the truck and moved over, ready for use.

"Have you got a telephone, son?" the foreman asked. "I've got a couple of calls to make."

I took him into our house to make the phone calls and on the way I said, "That culvert's too small anyhow. It gets blocked every time it rains, and floods all the lawns on this side of the road."

"I think there has been a complaint or two about that.

176

Well, I suppose we might just as well put in a larger one while we're at it." He looked at me and grinned. "How big a one would you suggest?"

"Big enough for me to crawl through," I replied. "Then if Agony gets stuck again I can crawl in and get him."

"That's an idea," he said thoughtfully. "I wonder why no kids have ever been stuck in a culvert. They've been stuck every place else."

After they had cut through the black-top they struck the softer dirt underneath. The power shovel was moved into position and it began digging. By two-thirty in the afternoon they had dug a big, wide trench and were only a few inches above the culvert. They dug down on each side of it until it was lying in the open at the bottom of a wide ditch. Next they dug a hole underneath the middle of the culvert, hooked a chain on it, and hooked that on the dipper of the shovel. A couple of minutes later the culvert was hanging in the air like a pencil tied to a string. It was almost perfectly balanced in the middle, and first one end and then the other would swing up. Agony was scared. He started howling like mad. I'll bet the late arrivals were puzzled to see that long culvert hanging in the air with those weird sounds coming out of it.

"Which end did he go in?" the foreman asked.

I showed him and he pushed down on that until the culvert was tilted up in the air at about two feet above the bottom of the ditch. Then two men banged on it with crowbars. Agony howled and they banged, and a minute later he came sliding out the lower end, followed by a whole mess of mud and leaves.

Everybody shouted in approval and I jumped down in the ditch to see how Agony was. Before I reached him he got to his feet and shook his head as though bewildered by it all. Then he scampered across through the trench that had been dug, headed toward Uncle Al's house. I thought he was scared and was getting out of there as fast as he could. Instead when he reached the other side of the road he began sniffing around the grass and bushes and then suddenly began baying and went kiting across the front yard. All of us stood staring after him in amazement.

"You say he chased a rabbit in there?" the foreman asked.

"Yes, the rabbit went on through."

"And out that end?"

"That's right."

The foreman shook his head. "Now that's a real hunting dog for you," he said. "He's trapped in a culvert for three or four hours and when he gets out what does he do? He picks up the trail and keeps right on going. Son, if you ever want to sell that dog, let me know."

The new culvert didn't arrive and at four-thirty all the men left, leaving their equipment parked beside the road. People who normally came home by our road found it blocked with a sign saying "No through traffic." They all had to detour about two miles out of their way. It seemed that everyone who lived in Grover's Corner itself came from the wrong direction. When they arrived at the trench they couldn't get across it to their houses. Most of them left their cars parked at a neighbor's rather than drive all the way around.

Uncle Al was lucky. He came home from the right direction and was able to get in his driveway. He parked his car and came over to where Midge and I were inspecting the road equipment.

"What's happening?"

"They're putting in a bigger culvert," I replied.

"How big?" he asked.

"Big enough for me to crawl through," I said. "At least when the man asked me what size I thought we needed that's what I told him."

Uncle Al seemed sort of weak. He leaned against the air compressor. "How did you manage it?" he asked. "Don't tell me you blew up the old culvert?"

"No, it was all an accident," I said. "Agony was trapped in it."

Between us, Midge and I told him the story. When we had finished, he pulled five dollars from his wallet and handed it to Midge. "He's the president of that research firm of yours and I suppose you're the treasurer. We didn't agree on any fee to solve this problem of getting a bigger culvert, but it's certainly worth at least five dollars to me and I've got to admit you gave me prompt service."

"But you don't owe us anything," I said. "It was entirely an accident. We didn't plan for Agony to get trapped."

"Maybe not," Uncle Al replied. "But you've got a way of making accidents happen. Here, take the five dollars."

Midge took the five dollars. "Hank did tell him that we needed a bigger culvert," she said, "so I suppose we earned something. We're going to get a cement one this time."

"As long as the man thought he could get Agony out by digging up the culvert I wasn't going to argue with him," I said.

Uncle Al looked at me suspiciously. "Did you have some other way of getting him out?"

"Yes."

"What did you mean when you said you weren't worried about getting him out?" Midge asked.

"Oh, I knew how to get him out of there," I said. "I figured that out just before they got here."

"How?" Uncle Al demanded.

"I was going to hook up the garden hose," I said. "I'd let the water run through the culvert and it would wash the dirt out. It might take an hour or two, but the mud in there was still soft. Agony might have gotten a little wet, but eventually he'd have been able to go on through."

Uncle Al ran his hand down over his face and walked off, muttering to himself. I don't know what was wrong with him. Maybe he thinks that wouldn't have worked but I'm sure it would have.

Tuesday, August 6th

The firm of Henry Reed, Inc., went into the mushroom business today. I doubt if you'd call hunting mushrooms research. Probably just plain ordinary search would be better. Whether it was research or not, it was profitable. Midge and I made about four dollars in about two hours and a half.

Aunt Mabel says it was the damp weather after a dry spell that caused the mushrooms to come out the way they did. She claims she's never seen them so plentiful before. They were growing all over our side lawn and out in the pasture behind Midge's house. We got a great big basket and filled it in no time this morning. Aunt Mabel went over all of them carefully to make certain that there were no poisonous mushrooms and then we divided them up into smaller baskets. She bought two baskets at fifty cents each, Midge's mother bought two, and altogether we sold eight right here at Grover's Corner. There were still plenty out in the pasture, but we had exhausted the market.

Agony was feeling fine today and doesn't seem to have suffered any damage from his afternoon in the culvert.

He went mushroom-hunting with us. Each time we picked one, he'd sniff at the ground where it had been broken off and start digging. He seemed to like the smell of them, so tonight when Aunt Mabel had some for dinner I gave Agony several in his dish. He ate them immediately and seemed to enjoy them.

After dinner I came upstairs and found a book on mushrooms in my mother's nature library. She had a twenty-volume encyclopedia on nature and about forty other books. I'd like to take them all back to Naples with me but it costs a lot to ship books back and forth across the ocean. That is probably why she didn't take them with her in the first place.

I read about how to tell edible mushrooms from poisonous ones and looked at all the pictures. It seems there isn't any foolproof way of testing mushrooms to make certain which are safe to eat. You simply have to know them. There are certainly more different kinds of mushrooms than I had any idea there were. I was thumbing through the book looking at the pictures when I came to a section on truffles. There was a picture of a man in France using a pig to find truffles. I once saw a man hunt truffles with a truffle hound in Italy, so naturally I read the article. It was very interesting and it gave me a wonderful idea. The author said that a few truffles had been found in America but that none of the really delicious ones had been discovered yet. He saw no reason why they shouldn't be

184

found in America, though, and believes that the man who finds them will probably be famous and will make a great deal of money. That decided me. Agony is not only a smart dog but he has an unusually keen nose. Since he likes mushrooms anyhow, he should make an excellent truffle hound.

Wednesday, August 7th

I told Midge about my idea today but she wasn't very enthusiastic. The main reason was that she didn't know anything about truffles. In fact she thought I said "trouble" at first.

"He's already a trouble hound," she said. "He doesn't need any training."

"Truffle," I said. "T-r-u-f-f-l-e."

"What do you do with a t-r-u-f-f-l-e?" Midge asked. "Wear it, look at it, or what?"

"You eat them," I told her. "That is, if you find very many of them you do. The first one or two we find will probably be preserved at some museum and we'll become famous as the discoverers of the first truffles in America."

"Columbus, Balboa, Lewis and Clark, and Reed and Glass," said Midge. "It sounds wonderful but you still haven't told me what a truffle is."

"I guess you'd call it an underground mushroom," I said. "They range from about the size of a walnut to a medium-sized potato. Some of the best truffles in Italy are white but all of them in France and some in Italy are black. What-

186

ever color they are, they're delicious and they are very expensive."

"All right, you've read a book someplace," Midge said. "Go on and tell me some more about truffles."

"Well, you train a dog, or in France they use pigs, to like truffles. He goes sniffing around over the ground and when he smells a truffle he starts digging. They say a pig can smell them farther than a dog, but the trick with a pig is to get the truffle before he does."

"How deep are they?" Midge asked.

"Oh, one foot, two feet," I said. "You usually find them under oak trees."

"It sounds like a lot of work," Midge said. "I wonder if it'd be worth the truffle." She started laughing as though she had said something really funny. She's a real self-panicker.

"I think Agony would be a natural for a truffle hound," I said. "If any dog can find them he can."

"How are you going to train him?" Midge asked.

"I guess I'll let him smell a mushroom," I said. "Then take him out in the woods and see if I can't get him to locate a truffle. An ordinary mushroom doesn't smell nearly as good as a truffle, according to my book, but it's the best I have."

"What does a truffle smell like?"

"I don't really know," I said. "The author said one chef claimed they smelled like strawberries and another man

187

just said they have the most wonderful odor in the world. What we need is a piece of truffle."

"I'm going to Princeton right after lunch," she said. "There's a delicatessen on Palmer Square that has all sorts of fancy things. I'll see if they have any truffles. Even a canned truffle should be better than nothing at all."

I didn't wait to get the truffles but started training Agony that afternoon. I took him out on a leash in the woods and tried to put across the idea that we were looking for something buried under the ground. I think he knew what I wanted, and after I dug several holes he went sniffing around and dug some himself. We didn't locate any truffles, but then I didn't expect to right away.

While we were back in the woods I heard someone pounding over by Mr. Apple's. Agony and I went over to investigate. I was very careful to stay out of sight and to stay on my own property.

Mr. Apple was putting up a wire fence in the middle of his big back yard. He was using steel fence posts at least eight feet high and as near as I could figure out he was putting the fence around the same area that had been enclosed by the stakes and the rope.

He was doing a thorough job. He had dug a trench around the entire area, evidently planning on burying the wire in the ground at least a foot. A big steel gate was lying off to one side and there was a roll of barbed wire, I suppose to go around the top. There was no doubt about it,

188

he meant business. Either that fence was intended to keep in something dangerous like a tiger, or to keep out something dangerous like Midge or myself.

About four o'clock I was in the kitchen having a glass of milk when Midge appeared at the back door. She had a paper bag in her hand. "I couldn't get any plain truffles," she said, "so I got this."

I opened the bag and pulled out a small round tin. The label said "*Pâté de foie gras aux truffes.*"

"That cost a fortune," Midge said. "I don't doubt you when you say that truffles are expensive."

"*Pâté de foie gras* is expensive with or without truffles," said my Aunt Mabel, coming over to look at the can.

"And it's delicious," I said.

"You mean you've eaten this stuff?" Midge asked.

"Sure," I said. "I ate it in France. It's a liver paste with little tiny bits of black truffles in it."

"It's made from fat goose livers," Aunt Mabel said. "It's considered a great delicacy."

"The girl that marries him is going to have an awful time," Midge said. "He knows too much about food."

We opened the can and each of us had some *pâté de foie gras* on a cracker. Midge agreed that it was very good. She said that it tasted something like liverwurst, only much smoother and richer.

"I don't know whether this will work or not," I said. "These pieces of truffles may smell more like liver than they do like truffles. I suppose the best thing is to pick out all the pieces and then wash them off and see how that works."

It took us half an hour to separate most of the truffles from the *pâté*. There wasn't much more than a quarter of a teaspoonful when we finished. If you start with a small can of *pâté de foie gras* and there are only little flecks of truffles in it, I guess you can't expect to end up with much. Anyhow, we certainly didn't.

"Maybe I should string them on a silk thread and wear them around my neck like a necklace," Midge said. "They're worth more than diamonds."

We put the little pieces in a strainer and washed them several times in warm water. Then Aunt Mabel suggested that we boil them a little while in some water and put the water and pieces in a bottle, and Agony could smell that.

"Far be it from me to discourage anyone," she said. "But I've a strong suspicion that you've found all the truffles you're going to find right now."

We ate what was left of the *pâté* and decided to wait until tomorrow to start hunting truffles.

Thursday, August 8th

I think that Agony has the idea. I spent two or three hours with him out in the woods today. He likes the smell of truffles and he seems to know that I want him to dig for something. I think we're making progress, even if Midge doesn't. She watched us a while early this morning and then came back again about four o'clock this afternoon. Agony had located a spot that interested him underneath the big oak tree and he was digging like mad. Just as Midge appeared he dug up a bottle. He kept on digging, so I don't think that was what he was trying to find. Midge picked up the bottle and started laughing like an idiot.

"What's so funny?" I asked. Usually the things she laughs at aren't funny at all, but I'm always polite and ask.

"That's a cod-liver oil bottle," she replied. "What Agony smells is the liver instead of the truffles. I think he's doing a remarkable job locating a cod-liver oil bottle that way."

I took the bottle out of her hands and looked at it. "How can you tell it's a cod-liver oil bottle?" I asked. "It doesn't have any label."

"I recognize the bottle," Midge said. "It looks exactly like the kind my mother used to keep in the medicine cabinet."

Half the time I don't know whether Midge is kidding or not, so I didn't say anything. But I don't think Agony really did smell the cod-liver oil. I don't know what he was after, but whatever it was, we didn't find any truffles.

About six weeks have gone by since I advertised that I had found a beagle. I'd think that after that long a time Agony would legally be mine. I'll have to ask a lawyer about that. After all, I've spent a lot of time training him, which should make my claim better. A trained truffle hound is worth a lot more than just an ordinary beagle— not that Agony was ever an ordinary dog. I've quit worrying so much about someone claiming him since so much time has passed.

Saturday, August 10th

Agony still hasn't located any truffles. For the last two days we have spent most of our time hunting. We had gone over the woods at the back of my lot pretty thoroughly by the time I made my last entry in this journal on Thursday, the 8th. So Friday, Agony and I cut across the fields toward the woods that grow along Beden's Brook. Midge refused to come along. She says now that she thinks the whole idea is silly and that we'll never find anything except possibly a few worms.

It's probably just as well she hasn't been along because having a kibitzer around all the time is no fun. Also she has been able to keep an eye on the barn and has sold fifty cents' worth of worms.

Agony and I went up and down the creek and then we cut across the fields even farther to a big patch of woods over toward Mount Rose. We didn't find a thing but it wasn't such a waste of time as Midge might think. I saw three or four pheasants, a couple of mallard ducks on a little pool, and lots of squirrels, rabbits, and birds. I enjoyed wandering around through the woods and so did Agony. Today I took my lunch and spent the whole day there.

Although we took it easy and spent a good part of our time just looking around, we did hunt for truffles. I hate to admit it, especially to Midge, but I don't think we're going to find any. I've heard lots of people claim that America has everything. They're wrong. It doesn't have truffles. At least, this part of New Jersey doesn't.

About four o'clock this afternoon we were back by Beden's Brook near a small back road called Gilbert's Lane. Agony spotted a woodchuck and took out after him. The woodchuck went down a hole and for some reason or other Agony was determined to get him. Maybe all the digging he'd been doing for me made him think he was supposed to dig up woodchucks, too. I was in no hurry, so I sat down to watch him dig.

I guess he worked away for about fifteen minutes but naturally he didn't even get near the woodchuck. I could just see his tail sticking out of the hole, but a woodchuck burrow may go underground for fifteen or twenty feet. I know because I've tried to dig them up with a spade. What's more, a woodchuck can dig faster than a dog, and even if Agony had managed to get near him the woodchuck would simply have tunneled off someplace else.

I called to Agony and he backed out of the hole. I noticed a round black object where he'd been digging, and for a minute I thought maybe we had found a truffle. Truffles are sort of rough and warty on the outside though, and this was smooth. It turned out to be some sort of a

pot. It was really dark brown instead of black and looked
something like the brown baking dishes that my Aunt
Mabel uses for cooking macaroni and cheese in the oven.
There were some odd little zigzag decorations around the
top outside edge. There was only one chip out of it, so I
decided to take it home to use as a water dish for the
rabbit.

Midge was sitting in the barn at the desk reading a book
when I got back. She looked up and said, "Here come the

great truffle hunters." I didn't say anything, but started to wash off the old pot in a bucket of water we had for watering the rabbit.

"What have you got there?" Midge asked.

I decided to get even with her for making so much fun of me about the truffles, and I put on quite an act. I handled the bowl as though it were something very valuable and washed it very carefully. Then I dried it. "It's nothing at all," I said, "nothing important."

"If it's nothing important why are you being so careful with it?" she asked.

"I didn't know that I was," I said. But of course I had been. I took the bowl inside the barn and set it on a big shelf under the front window. Then I got two bricks and put them between the bowl and the edge of the shelf so that it couldn't possibly slide off. I really had Midge's curiosity aroused by this time. As she watched me she got more and more annoyed.

"Just what is so special about that old bowl?" she asked.

"Why, there's nothing special about it at all," I insisted. "I just don't want it to fall off that shelf and get broken."

"Well, it's certainly nothing pretty to look at."

I didn't tell her that the only reason I brought the old bowl home was to use it as a rabbit dish. I'll let her stew all night and tomorrow if she's a little nicer I may tell her the truth.

Sunday, August 11th

I didn't tell Midge about the bowl today. In fact, I don't think I ever will tell her. The whole business about that pot was an accident but she thinks I knew what I was doing all the time. Since she doesn't give me as much credit as I deserve for some other things, this will even things up. After all, my idea of hunting for truffles was a lot better idea than hunting for old pots. The only difference was that it didn't work. Any scientist has a lot of different ideas and he doesn't expect all of them to work, but Midge doesn't seem to understand that.

Aunt Mabel usually has her big Sunday dinner about two-thirty in the afternoon. After church this morning I changed clothes and went down to the lot with Agony. I walked back in the woods and took a look at Mr. Apple's fence. He has it completely finished now, and there it stands in the middle of his big lawn with absolutely nothing in it. If he had put it off in one corner and put a little house in it I might have thought it was for a dog, or, with a bigger house, for chickens, but this has nothing in it at all. The fence is high enough to be used as a pheasant run but I can't imagine Mr. Apple raising pheasants.

At the beginning I pooh-poohed Midge's idea about **Mr.** Apple but I have to admit that there is something mysterious going on there. While I stood looking through the hedge he appeared, dragging the hose. He turned on the water and started sprinkling the ground inside the fence. That just doesn't make sense. He can't even see that big back part of the lot from his house, since there's a tall hedge that goes across, dividing the front and back of the lot into two separate parts. I watched him for quite a while and he went all around the fenced-in area, sprinkling the ground through the holes in the fence.

Finally I gave up and started back through the woods. When I arrived at the barn there was a car parked beside the road and a man was talking to Midge. He was an odd little man wearing brown khaki trousers and a green sport shirt with big red flowers all over it. His face was sort of red and sunburned and he was bareheaded. The thing I noticed especially was that there seemed to be more hair growing from the tips of his ears than from his head. There were little white tufts of hair in his ears and then other strands growing from the edges. He said his name was Zinser.

"I stopped to ask about your pigeons," he said, "but now that I'm here I'm much more interested in that bowl there in the window. Where did you find it?" He talked in an odd sort of breathless way and his words half tumbled over one another.

"Over toward Beden's Brook," I told him. It was easy to see that he was quite excited about the bowl and so I didn't admit that I thought it was worthless. "It looked kind of interesting so I brought it home."

"You were quite right," said the man nodding his head up and down. "It's exceedingly interesting. Did you notice the decoration on it?"

"You mean the zigzag lines around the edge?"

"That's right," he said. "They're almost like a signature. Unless I'm mistaken, that bowl was made by one of the first potteries in New Jersey, at least one of the first ones in this area. I've been trying to locate the site of that pottery for ten years. I know from my research that a man named Flanders had a pottery around here and that he made ware and sold pottery both to the Indians and to the early settlers."

"How old is that bowl?" I asked.

"I imagine at least two hundred and fifty years old. It's not that the bowl is especially valuable, except as a museum piece to illustrate New Jersey's early industries. I happen to be writing a history of New Jersey's colonial potteries, so I'm particularly interested. Would you care to sell that?"

"Sure," I said. "I was just going to—ah—" I stopped just in time. A few words more and I would have let the cat out of the bag. Midge was standing by, and I could tell that she was quite impressed because she was quiet. I sort of grinned inside myself and tried to look wise. Midge is always saying that I haven't any sense of humor. For a few minutes I was tempted to tell her that the whole business of being so careful with the pot was all a joke so that she could see how wrong she was.

"I'll give you ten dollars for it," the man said. "I think that's quite a fair price, but if you prefer you can check with the State Museum in Trenton or the museum in Newark because I don't want you to think that I am trying to stampede you into selling something that is very valuable."

"Ten dollars sounds like a lot more than it's worth to me," I said.

"As part of the bargain I'd like you to show me where you found it," the man said.

I agreed to do that and he handed me ten dollars. I turned around and handed it to Midge as though money didn't mean a thing to me. "Put this in the treasury, will you, Midge?" I said. "I guess we made out pretty well hunting for truffles after all."

"Truffles?" the man asked. "Have you been hunting for truffles?"

"I've been trying to train my dog to be a truffle hound," I said. "We were out hunting truffles when I found that bowl."

"I've hunted for truffles myself," said Mr. Zinser.

I stuck my nose in the air and looked at Midge

triumphantly. "You see, there are truffles in America."

"A few belonging to the truffle family have been found," he said. "But none of the delicious kind that are found in France and Italy. The Indians here in New Jersey used to hunt a sort of truffle-like growth they called a tuckahoe, which means a round loaf or cake. I found a few of those. They're usually attached to the roots of trees in low marshy places about two feet below the ground. Some of them get as big as my head. They are white and very nutritious, but not very flavorful. However, I think searching for the real truffle around here is rather hopeless."

Midge stuck her nose in the air and acted as though she had scored a point somehow. I never said that I was certain there were truffles. If a grown man like Mr. Zinser, who apparently knew what he was talking about, thought there was a possibility of finding truffles, I don't see why it was so dumb of me to think so. Anyhow, regardless of what Midge thought, it was a relief to know that the reason I hadn't found truffles was not because Agony wasn't smart enough to find them.

It turned out that Uncle Al knew Mr. Zinser, so he, Midge, and I got into Mr. Zinser's car with him and we drove over to where I had found the bowl. Mr. Zinser looked at the woodchuck hole and then poked around in the weeds, getting more interested all the time. After he pointed it out, I could see that there were the remains of an old foundation there. He got a shovel out of his car and dug around and found three or four pieces from pots or jugs and two or three bricks. He was more excited every minute.

"I think without a doubt this is the site of Flanders' pottery," he said. "This is most interesting and I'm most indebted to you, young man. I plan to write an article for the historical society and I'll give you full credit for finding the site."

I told him that if he was going to mention me it was only fair to mention Agony, since Agony was actually the one who had found the bowl.

"You're quite right," Mr. Zinser said. "As a matter of fact, I'll say that you were searching for truffles and that your dog Agony is the only truffle hound in America."

He took us back home, since it was almost dinner time, and then drove off to ask the farmer who owns the land if it would be all right to do some digging. I guess he plans to spend most of next week digging over there. I hope he finds lots of pots.

Saturday, August 17th

It's been a very quiet week. I went over three or four times to watch Mr. Zinser digging where the old pottery is supposed to be. He seems quite satisfied and happy because he found a lot of pieces of pots and one or two jugs or crocks that were in one piece. They all looked pretty uninteresting to me, but I guess he likes them. My Uncle Al says you can mention most anything and sooner or later you will find someone who collects it. To prove his point he showed me an article in a farm magazine about a man who collects old steam threshing engines. He has them parked all over four or five acres of his farm. I guess Uncle Al is right. Midge's mother collects yellow dishes and bottles, which she calls vaseline glass. She seems to like it even if it is ugly, and there are lots of people who are crazy about stamps. I don't understand it myself. It seems to me that if you're going to be a collector you might as well collect something interesting, like animals or turtles or fish, or something that's alive.

Mr. Glass's Men's club had a charity auction last night and a sort of fair just outside Princeton. They had collected all kinds of stuff such as old furniture, dishes, books

—anything that anyone was willing to donate. Then an auctioneer sold all this to the highest bidder. They also had a number of stands where you could take chances on blankets, or win a clock or a doll or something just as useless. Mr. Glass worked in the balloon stand. He filled balloons with gas from a cylinder and another man sold them. Most of the kids lost their balloons because if you let them go they really went up fast. I bought one and tied a good-sized rock on it to see how much it would lift. I kept tying smaller and smaller rocks on the string and finally it got away and went up in a tree where it must have hit a sharp point on a branch. It exploded.

I asked Mr. Glass about the balloons today and he said that the reason they went up so fast was that he had filled them with hydrogen. They had a cylinder at his laboratory which they weren't using and he donated it to the fair.

"Hydrogen is the lightest gas known," he told me. "That's what they used to use to fill the big balloons for balloon ascents. Also they use it for dirigibles. Did you ever hear of the Graf Zeppelin?"

I said that I had read something about it someplace. "It burned, didn't it?" I asked.

"That's right. Hydrogen will burn. In fact, mixed with oxygen it practically explodes. The United States uses helium for its balloons. It's not quite as light as hydrogen but it's not inflammable and so it's much safer. Ordinarily when you go to a fair and buy inflated balloons they'll be filled with just the ordinary gas that you use in a cook-stove. That is mainly carbon monoxide, which is somewhat lighter than air. If you have a balloon like a weather balloon which you really want to go up high, it should be filled with either helium or hydrogen."

He put the cylinder in his garage when he came back from the fair and it's still about half full, according to him. I asked him what he was going to do with what was left and he said he supposed he'd take it back to the laboratory, because the cylinder or drum was worth something. He doubted if they would ever use the gas.

It seems a shame to waste all that gas and I think the Henry Reed Research Organization is going to have to do a little research on how to use it.

Monday, August 19th

Everything is working out fine. The firm of Henry Reed, Inc., is going to do space research. We've got all the material and I've figured out how to do it.

There was a lot of noise in the field out back of Uncle Al's house early this morning, so after breakfast I went out to investigate. Mr. Baines, who farms the land, was cutting the grass with a machine he calls a forage harvester. This cuts the grass and clover, chops it in pieces, and blows it into a big wagon. When he had filled the wagon Midge and I rode on it to the farm. There were two station wagons there and four or five men. They were from the Agricultural Experiment Station at Rutgers and they were working with Mr. Baines on a new method of making silage. They took the chopped-up grass and dumped it in great big plastic bags which they then sealed. They said it would keep inside these bags all winter if necessary.

The plastic bags were about ten feet long and at least four feet in diameter. They seemed quite tough. I asked them for one and they said if there were any left over I could have one, so I went back about five-thirty. They were gone but they had left a bag behind for me as they had promised.

A plastic bag like that will make a perfect balloon. I remembered reading an article earlier in the summer about a man who went up a long way in a balloon. I found the magazine and read the article again. Sure enough, his balloon was made of plastic, so my silage bag is going to be just what I need.

Tuesday, August 20th

I went to the library today and read everything that I could find on balloons. It seems the Army and Navy and Air Force and the weather service all use a lot of balloons. One of their troubles is that if they send a balloon up with instruments, such as thermometers and barometers, half the time they never get the balloon or the instruments back. Sometimes they send up bigger balloons with all sorts of complicated radio equipment which automatically sends back information. These are very expensive and if there's much of a wind they often lose these too. Then of course there are the biggest balloons, which go up with a gondola that will carry a man. Naturally they always take a lot of precautions with these because the men who go up want to come back in one piece. They object to being lost with the balloon.

I've thought quite a bit about it and I've decided that I could do everybody a great service if I could develop a medium-size balloon, say about the size of my big plastic silage bag, that would be very cheap but would carry some instruments which would always get back. I have what I think is a brilliant idea. I can send up homing pigeons in the balloon and they can fly back. Of course a pigeon wouldn't be able to carry a very heavy instrument, so any thermometers or barometers that were sent up with the balloon would have to be small enough to be strapped to the pigeon's leg, but if I can work out all the other details the armed forces ought to be able to figure out how to make small instruments.

A real trained homing pigeon would be best, naturally, but all pigeons tend to find their way back home. I don't intend to waste time finding just the right pigeon because I haven't got much time. I have to fly back to Naples next week. Uncle Al got the ticket today. There'll be just time enough for me to finish my experiments in space research with my plastic balloon. If my idea works, Henry Reed, Inc., should really be on the map. I expect I'll be made a lieutenant in the Army and Navy and at least a general in the Air Force.

I asked Uncle Al about the pigeons again at dinner tonight. He says they are all part homing or racing pigeons and probably would be able to find their way home from quite a distance. Anyhow, I'm sure they'll do and I'm going to slip over as soon as it gets dark and catch a good healthy one.

Wednesday, August 21st

I told Midge about my idea today and she thinks it sounds wonderful. She was a little doubtful at first that we would be able to work out all the details but before the day was over we had practically everything figured out. In fact, I think we should be able to send up our balloon tomorrow.

We did some of the preliminary work today. We took the pigeon that I caught last night and went down the

road half a mile with it, carrying it in a basket. Then we let it out. It flew straight back home. I'd put a red leg band around it so there wasn't any mistake. There it was sitting on top of the barn. If I can, I'll catch the same pigeon again tonight.

We found a round wicker basket in Midge's basement which Mrs. Glass gave to us. This afternoon I built a small slotted cage for the pigeon. It has a little door that slides up and down. The problem of how to release the pigeon after he has been up in the air for a while was a tough one. And for a while I didn't think we could solve it. Midge gave me the idea.

"We'll have to put the pigeon to sleep somehow," she said. "Then we can send an alarm clock up in the basket with him to wake him up after he's been up for say half an hour."

Of course she was just kidding but it gave me an idea. Aunt Mabel has an old-fashioned round alarm clock upstairs in the guest room. She didn't want to part with it at first but I offered to buy it and finally she gave it to me. When the alarm goes off, the little thumb screw or handle on the back that you use to wind the alarm goes around and around. I fastened a wire to this and a string to the wire. When the alarm goes off it winds up the string. The string runs over a pulley and is attached to the little door of my pigeon cage and it gradually raises the door. It looks sort of complicated and homemade but it works. Midge and I tried it three or four times and it opened the door every time. We are all set and tomorrow is the great day.

Thursday, August 22nd

We had the great balloon ascension today. The balloon went up and it came down. I don't know whether you would call it a success or not because it didn't work out exactly as Midge and I had planned. I don't think we will be as famous as I had hoped, but it isn't really our fault. Still I'm going to write the Air Force and tell them my scheme. Maybe they can try it out in the middle of a desert someplace where they won't be bothered by all the complications that we ran into. I guess the best way to explain just why the experiment wasn't completely successful is to tell everything that happened today.

It took us much longer to get the balloon ready than we had expected. There was considerable work and also we had some interruptions. We spent a good part of the morning chasing Mr. Baines's sheep. Mr. Baines had turned about thirty sheep into the pasture out back of my lot. They found a hole in the fence someplace. At least, eight of them did. We were busy working on the balloon, trying to attach the basket to the plastic bag, when suddenly these sheep walked through the woods and stood there staring at us. We thought we would chase them back

213

where they came from but when I went to look I couldn't find the hole. Maybe they jumped the fence, I don't know.

They weren't bothering us so we let them graze a while on the lot, but then they wandered out toward the road. Three of them started across just as a big green sedan came by. Grover's Corner is such a little place it isn't really a town at all, and a lot of people don't even slow down when they go through. This man must have been going sixty miles an hour and he missed those sheep by inches. He swerved and there was a screech of tires and his car rocked back and forth. He managed to get it under control again but it was certainly close.

We went across the street to Midge's house and tried to call Mr. Baines but no one answered the phone. I don't know whether he was away or out in the fields.

We went back to the lot to see what had happened to the sheep but when we arrived they had disappeared. We thought they had gone back where they came from but a few minutes later we heard a "baa."

"They're over at Apple's," said Midge. "I bet he loves that." The thought of it tickled her so much that she sat down and laughed about it.

I wanted to see exactly what he would do when he discovered the sheep and we took time out to go over by the hedge. The sheep weren't in the front yard so we went on back to where we could look into the back part of his lot. There were the sheep, all eight of them, inside the wire enclosure or pen that Mr. Apple had built. The gate had evidently been left open and they had simply walked in.

"I wonder why he hasn't noticed them," I said. "Usually he's out here with a cannon if a sparrow lands on the place."

"I know," said Midge. "They aren't home. I saw them driving out in their car right after breakfast this morning. She was all dressed up so I suppose they went to New York or Philadelphia or someplace to go shopping."

"If those sheep do wander into the front yard they'll eat all her flowers," I said. "Maybe I ought to slip over and close that gate. They can't do any harm in there."

"That's not a bad idea," said Midge, "but I think we ought to do it for Mr. Baines rather than for Mr. Apple. It will keep his sheep from getting killed on the highway."

I slipped through a hole in the hedge, walked across the lawn, and closed the gate to the wire pen. The sheep were busily eating and didn't bother to look up.

About eleven o'clock Midge went over to her house for something and she called Mr. Baines again. This time Mrs. Baines answered. Mr. Baines had gone with his hired man to some auction sale where he hoped to buy some dairy cows, and would not be back until later. She said he would be over in his truck to get the sheep as soon as he got home. That was settled, so we forgot about the sheep and went back to our balloon.

There's no use going into all the details with the troubles

we had getting the basket attached and getting my pigeon cage rigged up just right. We spent most of the morning at it and so it was after lunch before we went to get the cylinder of gas. This was too heavy to handle and I had to go back and get Uncle Al's tractor and cart.

We had quite a time getting the balloon inflated. I had read enough to know that you don't inflate a balloon all the way so that it's nice and fat like a sausage. Instead it should be only half full and look sort of limp. Then as it goes higher and higher the gas expands and the balloon fills out.

It took us half an hour to locate a hose to attach to the cylinder to use for inflating the plastic bag. Finally we managed it. About three-thirty we had the balloon inflated just right and it was tugging at the ropes. Everything looked promising.

I'd caught the same pigeon the night before and I got him and put him in the little slotted cage. I hooked up the alarm clock and set the alarm to go off in about fifteen minutes. I didn't have any instruments to strap to the pigeon's leg, but since this was just an experimental run we figured that wasn't necessary. The main idea was to prove that it would work. From the way the balloon kept tugging at that anchor rope there wasn't much doubt that it would work.

"What if it goes up too fast?" Midge asked.

"How can it go up too fast?" I said.

216

"Well, then, too far," she said. "Supposing it goes up so far that the pigeon can't breathe. Doesn't the air get thinner the higher you go?"

I had to admit that it did but I doubted if our balloon would get up that high. However, Midge kept worrying about it.

"Well, I'll tell you what we'll do," I said. "We'll put a couple of bricks in the gondola to add a little weight. We can let it go up a way on a rope to get an idea how far and how fast it will go up."

The trouble was that we didn't have a long rope. The balloon was tied with a piece of clothesline and that was only a few feet long. "A really good strong twine would do the trick," I said. "Do you suppose you could find a ball?"

"I think so," Midge said and started to go across the street to her house. She had gone only a few feet when she turned around and said, "What about witnesses?"

"What do you mean, witnesses?"

"We ought to have someone who sees all this and can swear to it afterwards. Even the Wright brothers had a few people watching."

I had to admit that she had a good point. The only trouble was that if we invited a lot of people over to see our great experiment and then it flopped, we would feel foolish, just as we had when they discovered that our oil well wasn't an oil well at all. I certainly thought it would work, but so did all those Air Force scientists when they fired their first rockets down in Florida. Instead they blew up. I didn't know what to do.

"I know," said Midge. "We can take pictures."

That was a wonderful idea, and we both decided to get our cameras.

It was about twenty minutes to four when I walked into the kitchen. Aunt Mabel had just taken some cookies out of the oven but I was so excited that I didn't wait to get one of them. I rushed upstairs, got my camera, and hurried back toward the lot. Midge was crossing the street as I approached and we reached the barn together. Agony as usual was tagging along with me.

We had tied the balloon out in the middle of the lot where it would be clear of the trees when it started up. There was a big stump there and I had driven a spike into this. There was a loop in our anchor rope and this had been slipped over the end of the spike. The wicker basket was about six inches off the ground, suspended by four ropes from the bottom of the plastic bag.

We stopped and took pictures of our balloon from several angles and then I found several bricks. Since I had put the pigeon in his cage, all we had to do was put the bricks in the basket and let it make an experimental flight tied to Midge's string. We walked up to it, neither of us suspecting a thing, and so we were both flabbergasted when we looked inside. There sitting in the basket was

Siegfried, the Apples' white cat. He had knocked over the alarm clock, upset the cage, managed to get the door open somehow, and had killed the pigeon. When he saw us he glared at us and started waving his tail back and forth as though daring us to take the pigeon away from him.

I've never seen anybody as mad as Midge was. She was so mad she couldn't say a word, which means that she was as mad as she can possibly get. She sputtered and stuttered and jumped up and down. I looked around for a stick. In the first place Siegfried is a big cat and I didn't want to tangle with him with my bare hands. And secondly I wanted the stick to give him a couple of good swats, but before I could find one Midge thought of something else.

"I hope you go up so high you never come back," she said, and she reached out and grabbed the rope. Just at that moment Agony either smelled the cat, or saw him, or heard him, or found out somehow what was going on. He came rushing up from behind me and made a leap. He landed in the wicker basket just as Midge pulled the anchor rope off the spike. Midge said later that she was in such a rage she didn't realize for a minute that Agony had jumped into the basket. By the time she did it was too late.

With both the cat and the dog, and of course the dead pigeon, in the basket, the balloon didn't go up very fast. There is really no excuse for my not having caught the anchor rope. I guess I didn't understand what Midge had done for a minute. By this time the balloon was quite a way up in the air. I rushed over and made a leap for the end of the rope but just missed it.

"Agony's in there!" I said to Midge.

Midge nodded dumbly. "Yes I know he is," she said.

We both stood there like a couple of idiots while the balloon kept getting higher and higher. We were sort of hypnotized and we stood watching as it kept moving on toward the tops of the trees.

I doubt if either Agony or Siegfried knew what was happening for the first minute or two. As the balloon drifted upward, for a while I could hear Siegfried spitting. Then he let out an angry yowl and a minute later there was a yip from Agony. I suppose Siegfried scratched him. Then Siegfried's head appeared above the edge of the basket. I think he was about to jump out but suddenly he saw he was up in the air and couldn't, and after that I guess he was just too terrified to fight Agony any more.

"What are we going to do?" Midge asked in a scared voice.

"I don't know," I admitted.

The balloon reached the level of the treetops and began drifting slowly over toward Apple's. Midge and I traipsed along after it. I don't know what we planned to do but I felt I had to trail that balloon and get Agony down somehow.

The balloon just missed the big oak tree and then went over above Mr. Apple's lawn. Midge and I followed as far as the hedge and stood looking through it. There was scarcely any breeze and the balloon moved very slowly. If Agony hadn't been in the basket it would have been a beautiful sight and I would have been proud of it. As it was I was just plain scared.

It drifted on with the basket swinging back and forth gently beneath the big plastic bag. Then it passed directly over the Apples' house. As it did Siegfried poked his head over the edge of the wicker basket and saw his chance. I'll have to admit that he is a pretty smart cat. He didn't hesitate but jumped. The basket was about eight feet above the roof but of course that was no jump at all for Siegfried. The roof is a steep, gabled slate affair and certainly not a very good place for a landing field. Only a cat could have done it without slipping down and over the edge. As it was, Siegfried very nearly lost his hold. He

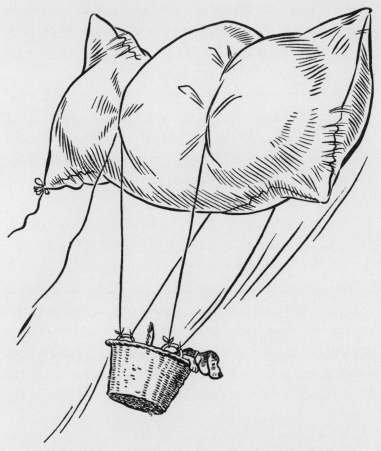

managed to get one paw over the peak as he landed. Somehow he pulled himself up and crouched there. He was
too scared to stir.

I suppose Agony wondered what had become of the
cat and he poked his head over the edge. It was the first
time I'd seen him since he'd jumped in the basket and I

imagine it was the first time he realized that he was up in the air. I would like to have seen the expression on his face. At the time, however, all I was worried about was that he might become panicky and jump.

"Stay in there, Agony," I shouted. "We'll get you down."

I didn't know how I was going to get him down but I was hoping. Up until this time Midge and I had followed along like a couple of big oafs, fascinated by that sight of that balloon up in the air, and not really thinking at all. Slowly we began to come out of it.

"Well, I might as well take some pictures," Midge said. "I guess Agony's on his way out into the great blue yonder. Maybe I can win a prize with my picture."

"I'm going to go see if somebody can't help us," I said.

For the first time I halfway wished that Agony's original owner would appear and want his dog. I would have been glad to see anyone who would help me get Agony back down to earth again. But no one did appear and I started running for home. At least I could ask Aunt Mabel for advice.

About halfway home I saw Mr. Ainsworth standing in his yard, looking up in the sky with a puzzled expression on his face.

"Is that contraption something of yours?" he asked.

I nodded. "It's a balloon, but my dog got in the basket by mistake and I've got to get him down!"

"Your beagle's in there?" Mr. Ainsworth asked.

224

Again I nodded. "Who do you think I should call? The state police? Do you suppose they could help me?"

"Maybe you'd better call out the Army and they could shoot it down." Then suddenly he grinned. "That's it," he said. "That isn't up so high. Maybe I can shoot it down for you. Come on."

We hurried to his house where he got out a .22 rifle. Then we got in his car and drove down the road. Midge was back by the road by this time and we picked her up too.

The balloon had drifted on and was over the middle of a big pasture beyond the Apples'. We got out of the car and hurried into the pasture a short distance. Mr. Ainsworth looked around carefully and then up at the balloon. "A twenty-two long will carry about a mile," he said. "I want to be sure where the bullet is going to land before I go firing up in the air."

I wasn't too keen on the idea of his firing that .22 in Agony's direction. "Are you sure you can hit the balloon without hitting the basket?" I asked.

Mr. Ainsworth looked at me and snorted. "Son, I've hunted ducks for forty-five years. I may be sixty-seven years old but my hand's still pretty steady. If I can't hit that balloon without killing your dog, then I'll take up knitting."

He raised his gun and fired. He waited a second and fired twice more.

"The trouble with this set-up is you can't tell whether you hit it or not. I think I've hit that bag but I'll give it a couple of more shots and then we'll wait and see what happens."

The balloon was still rising slowly and was probably another twenty-five or thirty feet higher than when it had passed over Mr. Apple's house. It was also drifting very gradually across the field. We followed a short distance behind. Mr. Ainsworth fired three times more before we reached the fence.

"That's got at least four or five holes in it," he said. "The trouble is that there isn't much pressure inside the bag to force the gas out."

"If the holes are up near the top, the gas will leak out," I said. "Of course it may take quite a while through little holes like that."

"All right, we'll make sure there's some near the top," he said, and he fired another three shots.

We all stood at the fence for several minutes, watching the balloon closely. When it had drifted almost to the far side of the next field, I climbed over the fence to go after it.

"I think it's settling a little," said Mr. Ainsworth. "It's certainly not rising any more. You go on ahead and follow it. I'll go get in the car and drive around and down Maple Road. That's straight ahead about three fields over. By the time it reaches that we should be able to tell what it's doing."

Mr. Ainsworth was right. It was fifteen minutes later before we were positive the balloon was settling, and I had to follow it about half a mile beyond Maple Road, but it did settle. Toward the last it came down rather fast and for a few minutes I was scared it would come down too fast and that Agony would be hurt. The basket landed with a bump but Agony jumped out uninjured. He was really glad to see me.

Mr. Ainsworth came up and together we examined the plastic bag. It was full of holes. I think almost every shot he fired must have hit.

"I'm certainly glad I found you," I said. "You saved Agony's life."

"I enjoyed doing it," said Mr. Ainsworth. "It isn't every day that a man gets to shoot down a balloon carrying a beagle."

Mr. Ainsworth dropped us off at the barn. There wasn't much left of all our equipment. The balloon was full of holes, the pigeon was dead, the alarm clock didn't seem to work any more, and the wicker basket hadn't been much good to begin with. Both Midge and I felt pretty discouraged.

"Some day I'll kill that cat," Midge said.

"Hey, what about the cat?" I asked. "Do you suppose he's still up there on the roof?"

We hurried over to the hedge and looked through. Siegfried was still clinging to the peak of the roof. He knew better than to move because those slates were slippery.

"How do you suppose the Apples are going to get him down from there?"

"I think they should get him down the same way we got Agony down," Midge said. "Shoot him down."

"The Apples still aren't home," I said, looking at their empty garage.

"They'll have a nice pleasant surprise when they do get back," Midge said and started laughing. "I'll bet that will keep Mr. Apple busy for a while—figuring out how that cat got up there."

It was a funny idea and we both sat down and laughed about it for a while. There just wasn't any possible way that cat could have gotten up there except by being dropped from an airplane or balloon.

"Don't worry," said Midge. "They'll blame us anyhow. Mrs. Apple will claim that you picked up the cat by the tail and threw him up there."

"I wonder how soon they'll be back," I said. "Sooner or later that cat will either try to make a move or he'll get so tired he can't hang on any longer. If he falls he'll be killed."

"Well, I'm not going to go over and hold a net and wait for him," Midge said. "I don't feel a bit sorry for him."

She did though, and we both got more and more worried. There was a big tree toward the front of the house and I had the idea that if the cat could be coaxed up in

228

that direction he might be able to make a leap into the tree. Midge and I walked out to the road to take a look. When we got there we saw that it would be a pretty long leap.

"They might stay out to dinner for all we know," I said. "They've been gone since early this morning."

"All right," Midge said finally. "I suppose we'd better call the Fire Department. I'll do it but I'm not going to say who I am, because whatever happens the Apples are going to be sore."

The hook-and-ladder truck arrived at about quarter to five, just when people began returning from work. Everyone thought there was a fire and stopped. People are naturally curious and I guess they would as soon see a cat rescued as watch a fire. Anyhow, inside of fifteen minutes there must have been thirty cars parked beside the road and there was a whole group gathered on Mr. Apple's lawn. Among them was Mr. Glass and my Uncle Al, but Midge and I stayed very carefully on our side of the hedge. We didn't see how anyone could connect us with that cat being on the roof, and we wanted to keep it that way.

The firemen got the ladder up and a man was halfway up to the edge of the roof when the Apples came home. Mr. Apple was too scared to be nasty at first. I suppose he thought his house was on fire. They got out of the car and one of the firemen told Mrs. Apple the cause of all the excitement. She looked up, and when she saw Siegfried on the peak of the roof she very nearly fainted. Mr. Apple and a fireman helped her over to a garden bench where she sat down.

"How do you suppose that cat got up there?" one of the firemen asked.

Mr. Apple just shook his head. We could hear everyone talking from where we stood at the hedge and they all seemed to be puzzled.

After the fireman reached the edge of the roof he still had to put up another short ladder and hook it over the peak in order to get to Siegfried. He finally did it, though, and Siegfried was so glad to get down that he didn't scratch the fireman.

Everything had gone very well up to this point. The Apples were acting almost human. Mrs. Apple was full of thanks to the firemen and Mr. Apple hadn't screamed at anybody for being on his lawn. A tall, sandy-haired man who had appeared with the Apples stood over by a lilac bush watching everything and saying nothing. Just when it appeared that all the excitement was over there were a couple of loud baas from the big back yard beyond the hedge. Midge and I looked at each other in surprise. Mr. Baines still hadn't come for his sheep.

Mr. Apple was surprised too, and then he was suspicious. He hurried over to the hedge and looked through the opening. From the bellow he gave you would have thought he was being murdered. He jumped up and down

230

and shouted something that I couldn't understand, and he looked as though he were going to have apoplexy. I guess everybody else thought the same thing and they all hurried over to find out what was the matter. Of course none of them understood why he was so mad and after they had looked through the hedge they still didn't know anything more than they had before. Midge and I hurried back to see what he would do. We arrived just in time to see him open the gate and rush inside his wire fence. He screamed and shouted and waved his arms. Of course the poor sheep were scared half out of their wits. They all rushed through the gate and went running out through the gap in the hedge into the front yard.

There wasn't much left of the grass inside the fence. After all, eight sheep had been there all day and they had had nothing to do but eat. It was cropped down almost to the roots. They had made a very thorough and very clean job of it. It wouldn't need mowing for a long time. Apple pointed at the ground, dancing up and down, and I wasn't certain whether he was going to cry or blow up. The sandy-haired man walked over, went through the gate, and stood talking with Apple for several minutes. Mr. Apple calmed down a little bit but he was still quite excited. The sheep went baaing off down the road but, as I said to Midge, I thought we had done our duty by them. It wasn't our fault if Mr. Apple let them out on the road to be killed.

Some of the people stood around a few minutes longer,

wondering what in the world had happened to Mr. Apple. However, there wasn't anything else to see. The fire truck drove away and soon everyone had gone home. It was dinner time so Midge and I went home too.

Aunt Mabel was home when I got there but she had been up to the road a few minutes earlier, watching Siegfried's rescue. Uncle Al didn't appear for another ten minutes.

"Well, that was quite a lot of excitement," Aunt Mabel said as we sat down to dinner. "How on earth do you suppose that cat got up there?"

"No one seems to know," Uncle Al said, looking at me. "However I was talking to Mr. Ainsworth just before I came in."

I could tell from Uncle Al's expression that he suspected something. After all it wasn't my fault that Siegfried had jumped in the basket and there was no reason why I shouldn't tell them what had happened, so I did. All the time that I was explaining things Uncle Al kept running his hand over his face.

"If I hadn't grown up with your mother I would swear all this was a dream," he said when I finished.

"What on earth was Mr. Apple screaming about there at the last?" Aunt Mabel asked.

"Oh, that," Uncle Al said. "That is the explanation of our little mystery about all his objections to trespassing. That tall fellow in the brown suit was Jim Weber. He used to be

232

county agent around here years ago, and now he's with a seed company in Philadelphia. I thought I recognized him and later on I went over and talked to him. That's why I was a little late getting back. It seems that Mr. Apple has developed some new kind of grass. Or at least he thinks he has. Now, this may sound ridiculous, but his grass is supposed to grow in a sort of a spiral. It's a curly grass and doesn't need mowing very often. He's got some idea that it's immensely valuable and it may be, although Weber says that such discoveries or developments never make a great deal of money. Anyhow, Apple has been working on four or five strains of grass and this is the one he considers to be the final answer. He thinks it will make him famous. He planted a plot in the back yard behind that hedge and put up a wire enclosure around it. According to Weber he's been so secretive and mysterious about it that it's ridiculous. I guess he was afraid someone would steal his secret. Anyhow, after a lot of negotiations and fiddle-faddle, he arranged for a seed company to send a representative up to see this great discovery. Jim Weber was the man they sent. The trouble is that when he did get out to look at it they found that some sheep had been locked up inside the enclosure and had eaten practically all the grass."

Uncle Al paused and looked at me. "How did those sheep get in there?" he asked.

I guess Uncle Al must be what they call psychic because there wasn't any possible way that he could know that I had anything to do with those sheep being in Mr. Apple's enclosure. "They got through a hole in the fence at the back of our lot," I explained. "Midge and I chased them and they went through the hedge into Mr. Apple's place. Of course that *would* be the only time that he ever left the gate open to his grass plot. I guess that grass must be good. The sheep went right in there and started eating it. I slipped over and closed the gate and Midge called Mr. Baines. We forgot all about them until we heard Mr. Apple scream. Besides we didn't know that was special grass."

"Well, Mr. Apple is very disappointed," said Uncle Al, "and I can't say that I blame him, but after all if he hadn't been so mysterious you'd have known that he was anxious to protect that grass and would have chased the sheep out instead of locking them in. Anyhow, Jim Weber told him this would be a good test of the grass. If it comes back it will be proof that it's tough."

Monday, August 26th

My vacation is just about over. As Aunt Mabel said it's been a quiet summer. There've been no boys around to play baseball with, and things like that, but all in all things have been fairly interesting. I've enjoyed running a business and I've had a good time with Midge, even though she is a girl with a peculiar sense of humor.

I have my tickets and Uncle Al and Aunt Mabel are going to drive me over to the International Airport tomorrow morning. Midge is coming along. I hate to leave but on the other hand I'll be glad to see my father and mother.

I went down to the barn this morning to sort of close up shop, since I won't be around to run Henry Reed, Inc., at least for a while. I'm hoping to come back next summer though, and maybe my father will get a tour of duty in the United States. That would be nice.

We drew our money out of the bank last Friday and divided it. We had almost forty dollars each, which proves that free enterprise is profitable. I went down to the barn this morning to dump all the earthworms and dirt out of the tub. The pigeons can go on living there just as they did before, and Midge can take her rabbit back.

235

It was about nine-thirty when I got to the barn, and Midge had a ladder up against the end and was painting out my name with red barn paint.

"What are you doing?" I asked. I didn't like that at all. Here I hadn't even left and she was painting me right out of existence. I thought she was going to put up her name. After all it is still my property, or at least my mother's property.

"I'm getting it all set so that you can paint the new name," Midge explained. "Reed and Glass Enterprises, Inc. We've got to hurry because Mr. Sylvester will be back about noon to take a picture of it for his newspaper."

"How come?" I asked.

"Well, he came by a few minutes ago to ask about our balloon experiment. I don't know who told him about it but someone did. I told him the firm name was changed and he promised to take a picture and publish it in his paper. After all, it's only fair for my name to be up there because I'll be the only one around to represent the firm, at least until next summer."

Agony had been sniffing around in the grass, and he suddenly let out a bay and started across the lot. By this time I not only know his rabbit voice but the special rabbit voice that he uses when he chases the white rabbit. I looked up and there was the white rabbit streaking across the lot toward the woods.

"You still haven't kept your part of the bargain," I said.

"You were to contribute a pair of white rabbits and one of the pair is still loose."

"The agreement was two white rabbits," Midge said. "Nothing was said about exactly what two rabbits or what size. I've kept my part of the bargain. In fact, I've more than kept it. Really, my name ought to be first, but I won't argue about that."

"What are you talking about?" I asked suspiciously.

"Go over and look in the nest box," Midge said.

I did, and there were eight baby rabbits. They were just beginning to crawl out of the nest. Midge hadn't kept her part of the bargain the way either of us expected, but she certainly had contributed more than two rabbits.

"All right," I said. "Where's the white paint for the sign?"

"It and the small brush are just inside the door on the table," Midge said.

I had to wait until about noon for the barn paint to dry and then I painted the new name, REED AND GLASS ENTER-PRISES, INC. I was sort of glad to see it go up. Then I painted a smaller sign on a piece of cardboard saying "Rabbits for Sale, 75¢" and Midge put this on a stick right beside the road.

Tuesday, August 27th

I'm writing this on the plane flying over the ocean. Uncle
Al, Aunt Mabel, Midge, and Agony all came to see me off.
Uncle Al and Aunt Mabel are going to keep Agony for me.
I doubt if anyone will claim him now, so he's mine for
keeps. Maybe I can get him sent to Naples but there are a
lot of customs restrictions and health requirements and
things like that, so he may have to stay until I get back,
which I hope will be next summer. Midge gave me a going-
away present—an enlarged picture of the balloon as it
went over Mr. Apple's house. Siegfried, the cat, was clinging to the roof and Agony was peeping over the edge of the
basket. It was a very clear photograph and it proves that
our invention will work.

Uncle Al said something peculiar just before I left. "Do
me a favor, will you?" he asked. "When Vesuvius erupts,
take a picture for me."

"Why?" I asked. "Do the volcanologists think it's going
to erupt?" The reason I happen to know such a big word
is that a very close friend of ours in Naples is a volcan-
ologist. That's a man who spends all his time studying
volcanoes.

238

Either Uncle Al knew the word or he figured out right away what it meant. "No, I haven't read of any predictions about its erupting," he said, "but *I* predict it will. With both you and your mother in Naples it's bound to."

I don't know what he was talking about and I don't think he does either, but, as I said before, sometimes I think he's psychic. I'm going to keep an eye on Vesuvius.